James R. Compton

Andersonville

The story of man's inhumanity to man

James R. Compton

Andersonville
The story of man's inhumanity to man

ISBN/EAN: 9783337367794

Printed in Europe, USA, Canada, Australia, Japan

Cover: Foto ©Andreas Hilbeck / pixelio.de

More available books at **www.hansebooks.com**

ANDERSONVILLE.

THE STORY OF

MAN'S INHUMANITY TO MAN.

BY JAMES R. COMPTON,

PRIVATE IN COMPANY "F," FOURTH IOWA INFANTRY.

DES MOINES, IOWA:
IOWA PRINTING COMPANY.
1887.

To the memory of that brave band of heroes who sleep the sleep that knows no waking, and who were true to the flag and the cause of freedom when the monster death was looking them in the face, is this little volume dedicated by one who suffered with them, but by the providence of God was spared to inscribe this tribute to their memory.

THE AUTHOR.

PREFACE.

Andersonville has become a part and parcel of the Nation's history, and in relating the experience of my incarceration and the consequent sufferings of myself and the brave boys in blue who were my constant companions in that hell on earth, it shall be done in as mild a manner as the thought of one who at this period of his life, after years of suffering from the inhuman treatment received at the hands of those in charge of that prison, can conceive. I shall not attempt to give the full story of the horror and misery of that vile abode, I merely give a sketch of my army and prison life, capture and escape, recapture by the rebel blood hounds and final escape from the most inhuman monsters that ever breathed the pure, free air of God, this little work is sent out with the hope that my comrades who have often recited the tale of war to their families and friends may thus have the history of that curse entailed by treason upon the brave boys who went down in the vortex, as a memento of one who was with them and who presents the story in its true light. It was through the heroism of those whose bones are bleaching under the rays of that Georgia sun and the patriotic devotion of their brave comrades who never faltered in their love for the flag and the cause of freedom, that their land is blessed with peace, plenty and happiness; and if we have said one word in this little book that will keep the memory of the dead bright and the cause of the living before the American people in its true light then our efforts have not been in vain.

Respectfully,

JAMES R. COMPTON.

CHAPTER I.

Enlists in the Army—Sent to St. Louis—A Dreaded Disease—General
Curtis Orders Medical Aid and Rations—Return to My Regiment.

FOR six years I had been a resident of Madison County, Iowa, when war was declared. The president, Abraham Lincoln, had called for volunteers. On the third day of July, 1861, William Debusk and I went together to Winterset, Iowa, and enlisted in the Fourth Iowa Infantry. Our captain was H. J. B. Cummings.

On the thirteenth of July we were taken to Council Bluffs to join our regiments, our neighbors using their teams to bring us to the Bluffs.

This was the first company which had left Winterset, and many affecting scenes were witnessed between parting friends. We were, for the present, stationed at Council Bluffs, Col. G. M. Dodge commanding our regiment. At the end of fifteen days' drilling a circumstance occurred to test the mettle of our recently made soldiers. It was reported that the rebels were encrouching on the Iowa line from Missouri; our colonel called for ten men from each company to go out and drive back the troops on the Iowa and Missouri line. The weather being very hot and the roads hard we were a sorefooted lot upon our return to our regiment. The visible forces in our front disappeared one night after trying to frighten us with a discharge of arms. Within five minutes after the discharge of arms by the rebs our column was in line of battle, but none of the boys were hurt. Soon after this we were placed on a steamer and taken to St. Joe, Missouri; from there to Hannibal and on to St. Louis, Missouri, where my trials began in earnest. Here we were all mustered into the United States service. At this time St. Louis was expecting an attack at any moment, large bodies of confederates being in that vicinity, so we were ordered to load our guns and to lay upon our arms all night. The following morning I found that I was unable to rise from my improvised bed, and was carried by my comrades to one of the hospital tents. Here I lay all that day and the following night wild with fever. During this day and night I was waited upon by Alexander Tedford.

When morning came again I discovered blisters upon my wrists and temples. At this time Mr. Banty, hospital steward, came in and asked me if I did not want to be removed to the general hospital, to which I replied that I did not unless some of my comrades could go with me to take care of me, to which he said I would be well cared for. Presently a team was rapidly driven to my tent door and two men hurriedly picked me up and tossed me into the wagon, bed and all. I said to them, you must be in a great hurry to get me away from here. I was driven away at a rapid rate. Your sick man could not comprehend why he should be hurried about in such a fashion, but presently we came to a wide road. On we went until finally we came to a beautiful shady place, with long velvety grass. Here we stopped and the wagon was delivered of its load. They next proceeded to pitch a tent. To my fevered brain it seemed that these preparations were for the purpose of burying me, but the men relieved my mind upon that score by telling me I had the small-pox, and in its worst form. After the tent was up they carried me in and placed me on the cot, and there I was left, it seemed to me, to die. I lay there for three long weeks in the care of two strange men from Co. B, of my regiment. I was supplied with neither doctor, medicine, food, and no instructions of any kind were left. Of course I grew rapidly worse under these conditions, the different pustules on my face coalesed, forming one covering of heavy exudation over the whole of my face. Sight was entirely gone for ten days. The two men who were left with me would only look in to see if I were dead. If dead, they would dig a hole in the ground and put me into it. These men were the two Bryant brothers, from Co. B. We were very hard pressed for something to eat; some potatoes and onions were donated by the citizens, and we traded a government ax for some apples and peaches. Some time had elapsed since I was put in the tent, and I had commenced to get better. Mr. Bryant reported our condition to General Curtis, which resulted in an order for us to be moved down the Mississippi river to the foot of those hills designated as Iron Mountains. General Curtis further ordered that we have medical attendance and plenty to eat, which was welcomed, I assure you.

The cause of my not receiving medical aid sooner, was of the report of our second surgeon, Dr. Grimes, to post surgeon when I was first taken ill that he did not consider my case a dangerous one; so when my regiment left, my surgeon paid no attention to me, which is the explanation of my being sick without medical attention. (This at least is the excuse the post surgeon gives.) I have learned that after my removal from my regiment, when my comrades learned of my condition, the officers were compelled to place a double guard around the regiment to which I belonged to keep them from coming out to care for me. But I presume it was better to keep them from me in order that the disease should spread no further.

In a few days the physician in charge told me that if I would change all my clothes and shave my head, and wade out into the river as far as I could, and wash myself thoroughly with soap twice each day for two or three days that I might then go to my regiment. That was joyful news to me. The expectation of again being with the boys filled me with happiness, for to me the regiment was home.

But there were places upon my face and hands which had not yet healed. Many persons were frightened at my appearance and would run away from me, as it was evident from my appearance what the trouble had been. To show how people feared the contagion of small-pox, I saw that all the passengers left the car on which I rode to Rolla, Missouri.

I left the cars at Rolla, Missouri, to walk out to the regiment, which was stationed at Camp Lyons. I was very weak and trembling when I left the cars, and my steps were very unsteady. My feet seemed to raise too high when I would step. The boys saw me coming, and some of them ran across the guard line to meet me, among which was George and Charles Tibbles, E. Decker, and others. They were rejoiced to see one whom they supposed was dead. What pen can picture the joy of such re-unions? Lieutenant Stitt laid hold of me and marched off to headquarters, where I enjoyed a bountiful repast with Lieutenants Stitt and Goshorn, which consisted of peach cobler and other good things. C. E. Tibbles took occasion to remark that he was going to sleep with me that night. This was followed by objections of others who claimed the right, but as C. E. Tibbles had always been my bunk mate it was decided in his favor.

Dear reader, do not think that the boys all wanted to bunk with me because I was so handsome, although Dr. Grimes always denominated me by "pretty" after my return. No, it was that feeling that one soldier boy has for his comrades in hardship and danger. At this time our camp was situated one mile south of Rolla, on a beautiful elevated spot of ground. Here we remained for some time. The usual routine of camp life, drilling, picketing, scouting and guard duty kept us here until we drew our first pay from the government, which was in gold, silver and greenbacks. This was all the hard money paid to us during the war. A portion of our time was made to pass more pleasantly by several temperance speeches, notable among which was one delivered by Rev. Storrs, of Winterset. These exercises were very much enjoyed by the boys. About this time we moved our camp down to Rolla, Missouri, where we built our barracks for our winter quarters.

CHAPTER II.

Improvement in Health—Foraging for Stock—Measles in Camp—The
March on Springfield, Missouri, and its Capture—Description of
Pea Ridge.

MY health was very good now, and I became very stout again.
I would volunteer to go with every scouting party that
was sent out.   At one time there was ten out of each
company asked to volunteer to go on a scout some distance
from camp.   I was one of the number from our company.
We started out and went south from Rolla about twenty-five
miles to a little village called Licking.   Here a captain was
detached with each squad and we started out.   We employed
skirmishers and coralled the whole country.   We were ordered
to let nothing pass through our lines.   The first our squad
found was a man with a number of horses.   Our commander
called to him to halt, which he immediately obeyed.   We took
the horses.   Our next conquest was a large Texas steer, which
I had the honor of downing myself.   When we all came
together we had a large drove of animals.   We had some
nice sheep, cattle, mules, asses, and other things too numerous to mention.   We finally started for camp, and when the
boys saw us coming they thought we were a large band of
Mormans or Gypsies on the war path, when finally they concluded it was the whole southern confederacy coming down
upon them.   We boys had our fun as well as doing good service for the government.   Elihu Debusk died in this camp
with measles, and his father Isaac took his place in the company.   Also another one of the same family by the name of
Levi Debusk was discharged and sent home sick before we

left Iowa.   We were all getting very anxious for active service
and wanted a brush with the rebs.

In February, 1862, we were ordered to march on Springfield, Missouri.   The state of the weather was decidedly bad
for the movement of an army.   There was snow, rain and
mud.   Within a few miles of Springfield we were met by a
regiment of Price's infantry, and a battery.   This movement
of Price's seemed to be for the purpose of covering his retreat
from the city of Springfield.   Price believing the whole Union
force was upon him, precipitately fled Springfield in the
night.   Lieutenant Stitt was detailed the next morning with
one company to ascertain, if possible, the situation of the
rebels.   Lieutenant Stitt was a fearless officer and man, whose
actions were ever guarded with caution.   With his detail he
cautiously approached the city.   He soon saw the city was
evacuated.   Pressing forward he succeeded in capturing a
number of rebels and some property.   When the main body
of the army arrived in the town Price was on the move—
retreating as rapidly as he could move his army.   We made a
close pursuit, and our troops were engaged almost every afternoon for several days.   We would press forward through
creeks, mud or snow upon the double quick to reach his rear,
when we would engage them.   Our men often caught chickens
which they would carry with them, and would be loth to let
them go even during one of these engagements.   I remember
very distinctly of dressing a goose on one of those afternoons,
and I thought it the best I ever ate.

We drove Price to Arkansas.   We now stopped several days
and drilled; also run a grist mill.   We were a tender-footed
lot of soldiers when we were ordered into camp.

At this place we received very strict orders, while on picket duty. One night when company F was on guard at the old mill, the snow coming down in great sheets, mixed with rain, I was stationed some hundred paces from the mill at the forks of the road. One of these roads led to our camp and one to Huntsville. There was a bridge on one road which I was to guard by hearing; the other I also had to guard. I was stationed in the shadow of some bushes about twenty feet from the bridge in such a position that I would not readily be discovered. The snow was still falling at 10 o'clock, and melting as it fell. About this time I heard foot-steps on the bridge. I expected an enemy, and hastily fixing bayonet I passed rapidly to the bridge, and with cocked gun I halted the man and demanded the countersign, which he gave correctly. This man proved to be a courier with a dispatch to Capt. Cummings. He informed us that the rebels were about to surround us. The army were then on the move, and he was to pilot us through the country by an old road to meet the main army. We arrived at the main road before the rebs did. Gen. Curtis was made to give the countersign. We marched all night in a snow storm. Men would fall asleep while marching along, and be awakened by falling in the mud, and still we struggled on until daylight's beautiful aurora began to show in the east when we were allowed twenty minutes to make coffee. We then marched to the top of the hill, when we stacked arms. Here we made some more coffee. Just as we got our coffee made, the long roll beat. We were in line almost instantly. From there we double-quicked to the Elkhorn Tavern. Here men came riding in hot haste with information that the confederates were moving. Gen. Curtis was quick to act. He must concentrate his forces. Cavalry men were sent across the country to officers who were out foraging; also to Sigel. Gen. Curtis resolved to fight a battle, although the rebels outnumbered him two to one. He selected Pea Ridge as his battle ground. To understand how the battle was fought let us first take a walk over the ground, starting from Elkhorn Tavern.

The road from Springfield to Fayetteville runs southwest. The tavern is on the ridge going down the road southwest. We then pass Sugar Creek. We come next to the hamlet of Mottsville, where the tents of the third and fourth divisions are standing. The valley is half a mile wide. Walking on we ascend another hill. Ten miles bring us to Cross Hollows, a place where the hollows or ravines cross each other. The ravines are narrow; about seventy feet wide; the banks steep, and the position one of great strength. Just south of Cross Hollows Gen. Van Dorn pitched his tent. Here we turn northwest, which takes us into Osage Springs, thence north to Bentonsville, which is ten miles west of Mottsville. Here we see the first and second divisions under Sigel. Turning now northeast we come, just before reaching Sugar Creek, to a road branching to the right. If we follow it we will come to the hamlet of Lee Town, and it will bring us back to Elkhorn Tavern. Following the main road we cross Sugar Creek and ascend Pea Ridge and come out to cross Timber Hollow, which is four miles due west of the tavern. Now, keeping these points in our minds we shall see how the confederates moved to surprise Gen. Curtis. Gen. Curtis had formed his line facing south, expecting that Van Dorn would advance from Cross Hollows, but that was not Van Dorn's plan, as we see him come up the road toward Gen. Curtis with a small force, while the main army turns west toward Ben-

tonville to meet Sigel. Messengers here brought word to
Sigel to retreat to Pea Ridge. He has two hundred wagons
which he sends in advance. The rebel cavalry meantime ride
rapidly around him and gain his rear, but he fights his way
through them, loosing twenty-eight killed and fifty prisoners.
He joins Curtis, who seeing Van Dorn's intention quickly
changes his front to meet Van Dorn's main body.

The Union line of battle, on March 7th, at Pea Ridge, was
as follows: Carr's division up the road to Elkhorn Tavern.
This division to hold the right of the line. They are in the
thickest of the fight, which is around the tavern. Next is
third division, under Gen. Davis. Beyond him, third and fourth
under Sigel.

The confederate line, Gen. Price with the Missourians, has
led the advance of the confederates, they having made a long
march and reached the road northeast of Elkhorn Tavern,
and confront Gen. Carr's division. Next in line toward Cross
Hollows are the Arkansas troops under Gen. McCulloch, while
the Texans and Louisianians confront Sigel.

CHAPTER III.

Pea Ridge—First Day's Fight—Loss of Federal Battery—Gen. Curtis'
Retreat Cut Off—The Out-look Gloomy for the Union Forces, when
Rebels Scatter and Run—The Victory Ours.

IT was 10:30 in the morning when Col. Osterhaus with
the Third Iowa Cavalry, a detachment of the First Missouri Cavalry and the Twenty-second Indiana Divisions,
Peoria battery advanced to reconnoiter the confederate position. The cavalry drove in the confederate pickets, the Peoria
battery opened fire, the pickets retreated to the woods, and the
cavalry charged after them. Suddenly the woods were thick
with confederates, the cavalry was driven back, while the confederates rushed upon the battery and captured two guns.
They were wild with joy. At the same time there was a ripple
of musketry in the woods north of the tavern. Pike was
advancing to attack Carr. The Union pickets were falling
back, the battle was raging so furiously on the left that Gen.
Curtis sent Gen. Davis to assist Osterhaus. The third division went through with his second brigade, commanded by
Col. White, Ninth Missouri, Thirty-seventh Illinois, and a battery of four guns. The brigade formed in line. The woods
in front of the troops were alive with Indians, under Gen.
Pike and the celebrated chief, John Ross. The Texans and
Louisiana troops charged upon the brigade with fury and were
driven back, and then the confederates with wild yells pierced
the air. They thought they were going to have things their own
way. The First brigade swept in, firing terrific volleys, in

2

which Gen. McCulloch was killed and Gen. McIntosh wounded. Backward and forward, over the knolls, through the hollows, in the fields and thickets, swayed the battle. Sigel's troops came in, Van Dorn ordered re-enforcements. Gen. Davis saw that the confederate's left flank was exposed. and sent the Eighteenth Indiana to attack it. The regiment fell like a thunderbolt upon the Indians, driving them and strewing the field with killed and wounded; rushing upon the cannon, wheeling them into position and turning them upon the fleeing confederates. The battle on the left center was over around the tavern and to the east of it. Col. Carr placed the first brigade.

Capt. Jones' battery was the first to open fire. Col. Vandover was at Huntsville, forty miles away. When Gen. Curtis' orders reached him the brigade had marched the distance, stopping three times, only making a rest at each halt of fifteen minutes. We see the brigade advancing half a mile north of the tavern, and Capt. Hayden's battery from Dubuque coming into position and opening fire. Sterling Price, commanding the Missouri troops, determined to strike with all his force. He presses on, drives Vandover towards the tavern, makes a sudden rush capturing one of the cannons.

Gen. Carr is out-numbered two to one. "I must have reinforcements," is his message to Curtis. "I send you my body guard; you must hold them," was the response, and Maj. Brown's Battalion of Cavalry went thundering down the road with a howitzer. They were all the troops that could be spared till the matter was settled on the left. "I cannot hold on much longer," was the second message from Carr. "You shall have help," was the reply, and a battery came up from the left, with a battalion of infantry. A few minutes later Curtis himself, with Arboth's division, came sweeping over the ridge to Carr's aid. Through the afternoon Price had passed on, Carr disputing every inch of ground; he had been driven a mile. Arboth's batteries wheeled into position south of the tavern. The battle was raging furiously; four men that stood next to me were shot; large trees were shot down with cannon balls. We had fired away all of our ammunition, so we charged bayonets and drove the rebs and held the ground till night. The battle being on the left, more of Sigel's troops come hurrying across the pasture. Night came on with the rebs defeated on the left, but well satisfied with what they had accomplished on the right; there they were in possession of the field, had captured our cannon, and had possession of the road to Springfield, cutting off Curtis' retreat. The outlook was not encouraging for Gen. Curtis, for when the sun goes down his line of retreat is cut off.

Second day—eight o'clock, and the confederates have not advanced. Gen. Curtis resolves to commence the battle. Sigel pushes his infantry forward, attacking the flank of the confederates. I will not narrate all the details; how Pattison's brigade and the Tenth Indiana Battery fought in the fields south of the tavern and east of the road; how the confederate batteries opened upon them, compelling them to fall back; how White's brigade and Davidson's battery made the line a sheet of flame on the left, and the Twelfth Missouri, with twelve guns, on the right in their rear, the men lying down and the cannon sending a storm of shells, into the confederate's line silencing Van Dorn's batteries, discouraging his troops, the Indians fleeing, the Arkansas and Louisiana troops loosing heart, the confederates firing grows fainter, the troops fleeing at last in dismay in every direction so suddenly that Gen. Curtis is at a loss which way to turn in pursuit. Eight miles away Van Dorn gathered a portion of his scattered troops, and sent a request to Gen. Curtis to bury the dead and care for the wounded.

CHAPTER IV.

After the Battle—Hospital at Springfield—Fishing and making Rings
of Mussel Shells—Trading Guns—Copperheads at Home

WE remained here in camp a few days and cared for
our sick and dead and wounded, and gathered up some
forage, moved our camp, and got our pay. I was now
sick with intermittent fever, but we started on a march
through Arkansas. But sick as I was, the captain told me
I must go on the march also. Colonel Dodge was here pro-
moted to brigadier-general, and Adjutant Williams was elected colonel of the Fourth Iowa Infantry. We now started
on the march. I was so sick and weak I could hardly walk
and it was ten o'clock at night before I got to camp. I was
so sick the next morning that Lieut. Stitt took Decker,
Logan, Keffer and me to the hospital at Springfield, Mo.

When able to travel again, we got a pass to Rolla, Mo.,
which was about sixty miles from Springfield. We stopped
at Rolla, rested, and had some fine times, then went with
some teamster to our regiment. On our road there we had
a good time. We would stop and take dinner with our Arkansas friends. When we got to our regiment at Jackson-
port, Ark., we remained there a few weeks, and spent our leis-
ure time fishing, bathing and making finger-rings out of mussel shells.

We then started on the march again for Helena, Ark. On
the road there we had several skirmishes with the rebels. We
marched on and on, and it being very hot, dry and dusty, we
had a long, hard march of it. It being almost impossible to

get water we nearly famished. We often used water with a thick green scum over it, and was glad to get that. One day while the dust was rising so thick that one comrade could scarcely see what the rest were doing we came upon a spring of good water. I rushed up to the fence that was around the spring, set my gun down until I could get a drink, and when I turned to pick it up again my nice gun was gone, and in its place an old gun, its stocks all split, and fit for nothing. Having a skirmish with the rebels almost every day, and I without a gun and could not get one honorably, I waited, thinking we would get into a general engagement, and I thought that perhaps I could then pick up a dead man's gun that might fall by my side. We had no chance to draw clothing, nor had not had since leaving Rolla, Mo., before the battle of Pea Ridge, therefore we were very destitute of clothing, and when we got to Helena, Ark., we were ragged and footsore. I firmly believe that when we got to Helena that there were five hundred of Gen. Curtis' men destitute of pants. So we drew clothing, and the lieutenant told me I had better draw a gun, but he said it would cost me $15. I told him I would not draw a gun. He said he would have inspection in the morning, then what would I do? The Government was issuing guns to some other soldiers, and when they got what they wanted and went away, I went up to the box and picked myself out the best gun I could find and took it, for I didn't think it right for me to have to pay for a gun when a soldier got mine, and I was working for the Government. But everything worked together for good, and I came out on inspection with flying colors.

We had been at Helena but a short time when the boys begun to get sick. I begun to shake with the chills and fever myself, and had them for three months every day, and became very weak and reduced in flesh. During that time I frequently received letters from home, stating that the copperheads, or "Southern Sympathizers," were riding around my father's farm and cheering for Jeff Davis. How that made the blood boil in my veins. Therefore I went to the captain and told him I would give him $50 if he would give me a leave of absence for one week so I could go home, for I wanted to put those rebels out of my father's way so they wouldn't bother him any more. But I could not go. I wrote a letter to one of them, and told him how I loved him, and what he was, and what he would bring himself and family to if they still remained enemies to our country; and he took offense at it, and had the letter published in the Winterset paper, and I will here state what the editor says about it:

"We insert the following by request of one Mr. B., whose object in its publication we know not, but we do know that the author of it is a soldier of Co. F, Fourth Regt. Iowa Vols., and that he is a truthful and an upright young man, therefore we cheerfully give it a place in our columns. Read it everybody. It is the best we have seen from the front lately."

This enraged the copperheads, and the editor was compelled to be constantly on his guard. I wrote this letter on the twentieth of October, 1862.

CHAPTER V.

Down the Mississippi—Arkansas Post—Council of War at Millikin's
Bend—Captured—Paroled—Benton Barracks— Memphis, Corinth,
Iuka—Rebels in the Blue—Death of James Stafford—Chickasaw
Landing—Battle above the Clouds—Tibbles as a Forager.

WE now had orders to proceed to Vicksburg, Gen. Sherman in command. We boarded a Mississippi steam-
boat and proceeded down the river to the mouth of the
Yazoo. We went up the Yazoo about ten miles and disembarked on the right bank. Our gunboats had the day previous
attacked Haines' Bluff, about twenty miles from the mouth of
the Yazoo river. Upon landing we were formed into line of
battle. The generals commanding were A. J. Smith, M. L.
Smith, Steele, and G. W. Morgan. We were about a mile from
the enemy's lines. In our line of advance the roads had been
destroyed, obstacles of all kinds strewed in our way, and progress was impossible. Gen. Sherman desired us to push to the
bluffs, but this was impossible through such obstructions as
we encountered.

At 8 A. M. 150 guns opened upon the Confederate position,
and for hours rained shot and shell upon the bluffs. From
bush and rock, tree and hummock, there appeared, as if by
magic, the rebel infantry. These troops exhibited great courage
and determination in their charge. The Federal troops here
charged the rebels, driving them back to their very rifle pits
where they were protected from our fire by pits and barri-
cades, but we were compelled to fall back. We had fought
our way to them through a murderous fire; a rain of shot and
shell, but no material benefit was obtained by this charge.

We left the ground covered with our dead and dying. The Fourth Iowa lost 120 killed and wounded in fifteen minutes in this engagement. Immediately after this charge there was a terrific rain storm. Among the killed of the Fourth Iowa was Lieut. Pitzer, Alexander Tedford, and Alfred Kelly; Fletcher Smith lost his arm. All these were from Co. F.

We were, soon after this battle, served with orders to fall into line and march to the fleet. None were allowed to speak above a whisper, nor to make any noise whatever. At last we were all aboard. The fleet immediately proceeded down the Yazoo river, bound for Arkansas Post on the Arkansas river. There was a council of war held at Milliken's Bend. It was decided to attack Arkansas Post. We disembarked about ten miles from the post. Our forces were so arranged as to almost surround the place. Our gunboats and batteries opened with terrific effect, mowing down the enemy in piles. One shell from one of our gunboats disabled their 160 pound cannon, and killed sixteen men at a single shot. When a solid shot could be put in lenghtwise of the rifle pits it would tear whole lines to atoms. We were close upon their works, and had prepared for a bayonet charge, when they ran up the white flag. We immediately entered their works taking 5,000 prisoners. Upon entering their works we gazed upon a sight of horror not soon to be forgotten. The dead and dismembered humanity; the dim and dying eye, in which the pictures of the battle still lingered; the boy of tender years, the gray-haired soldier, the mother's hope, the father's pride, in one red burial blent.

But to resume. There were other posts taken while we were at that place—St. Charles and Duval's Bluff. After this the main body returned to Vicksburg. My health at this time was not good, having been under the doctor's care a greater part of the time since I was sick before. My appetite was capricious—nothing seemed to taste good, so with another soldier I thought we would go a short distance and try to get a chicken. We had not gone far when we came upon some rebs who made prisoners of us. They were very much enraged, and we thought they would shoot us, but they finally concluded not to do so, but took us to Little Rock, Arkansas, where we were paroled, which no doubt saved my life; being much reduced in strength I could not have stood their treatment long.

After being paroled I was sent to Benton barracks, St. Louis, where I was soon taken with lung fever, from which I recovered in due time.

I now obtained a leave of absence and returned home, where I enjoyed my visit very much. Upon my return to my regiment I felt much stronger. During this stay in camp the boys would amuse themselves and employ their idle time in making rings of mussel shells, and other material suitable for the purpose. We could dispose of our shells for from fifteen cents to one dollar each. I also read the New Testament through at this time.

On the first day of October, 1863, I went to the front. Upon our arrival at St. Louis we found the boat was not ready to go. We returned to our barracks and remained that night. The following morning we left by boat for Memphis, Tennessee. On our arrival at Memphis we remained one day with the invalid corps. Then we were ordered to Corinth, Mississippi; from here by rail to Iuka, where I found the boys all right. We soon passed on to a station about forty miles distant called Cherokee Station. While here C. E. Tibbles,

Samuel Wilderson and myself were successful in foraging for food, getting an ample supply.

This was wet weather and we were thankful to be in a dry place. One day as we were about eating our dinner the long roll sounded, which was the signal for immediate action; we fell into line. The rebs had charged our camp and were now entering it. The reason of this surprise was that the rebels had donned the blue and we at first thought they were our men. W. Crandall said, "don't shoot them, they are our own men." Just at this moment the rebs opened upon us—killing James Stafford. Now that we discovered their identity we charged them and drove them about four miles through a drenching rain; after which we returned to camp. This shows the subterfuge which the rebels were always ready to use. Give me the manly, upright foe, not the one skulking under the cloak of friendship—until he can strike his unsuspecting foe. The next day after this occurrence we were ordered to prepare for a march. The next day we proceeded in the direction of Tuscumbia, Alabama. About 3 o'clock this day we engaged the enemy. The engagement continued throughout the day, and tired and weary we went on picket duty that night. The next morning we opened on the rebels with two parrot guns, followed by a dash. They retreated toward Tuscumbia, Alabama, that night. We returned the next day to Cherokee Station. On the following morning early we were attacked by a large force of rebels before we were out of bed. We soon formed and drove them back twelve miles. This engagment was in rain and mud. We marched on fifteen miles further to Chickasaw Landing, where we encamped. Here we were mustered for our pay. After this we were marched to Fayetteville, Tennessee. This was a hard and fatiguing

march. We halted and camped for a few hours at each of
the following places on our march: Maysville, Alabama, Bel-
mont and Stevenson, Alabama, and on to Bridgeport. We
camped here. Then crossing the Tennessee river we left our
teams at Shell Rock. Now we marched on around Lookout
Mountain to within sight of the enemy's rifle pits.

When we received our sixty rounds we were convinced some
one would be compelled to die. The next morning at daylight we formed in line of battle; Gen. Osterhaus was in command of our brigade. We marched on as if we intended to
march into the rebel rifle pits, but we stopped about 100 yards
from their lines and remained there until about noon. We
were placed there to draw the attention of the rebs from
Sherman until his right wing could surround them. We
then charged, taking 250 prisoners. We then charged Lookout Mountain and fought until about 1 o'clock at night. It
seemed to us we were above the clouds. The rebs rolled large
stones down the mountain at us. It was raining below us,
and boulders from above. Here would come the great boulders down the mountain side, accompanied by a streak of fire.
Large trees were crushed off like straws. These boulders were
accompanied by lead and iron hail.

Our division moved down the mountain that day, driving
the enemy before them, finally reaching the enemy's pits. Here
we took them lengthwise. A terrible fire was poured out by
both armies. General Grant now ordered Thomas to advance
and take the rebel rifle pits at the base of the mountains.
Sherman was then driving the enemy in great confusion, and
as General Thomas drove them out of the rifle pits they continued falling back through a gap at the foot of Lookout
Mountain and Mission Ridge, but we got into the gap first

and cut them off, capturing a lot of prisoners and guns. I was then sent back with some prisoners some six miles from the battle field, and even there it seemed terrible. Thousands upon thousands of muskets firing volley after volley at each other, and the artillery was so heavy and repeated so rapidly that the earth six miles away was all in a tremble. It seemed far worse to me there than when I was engaged in the fight myself. General Bragg's army and Hardee's command all fled, routed completely, toward Ringgold. Thousands of prisoners, and small arms and a large quantity of ammunition were taken by us from the confederates; Hooker pursued, and that night Mission Ridge blazed with Union camp fires. On the 26th of October I took the prisoners left in my charge to headquarters, and then went to my regiment, which was now some ten miles in Georgia, and the next morning being the 27th of November, we again made an attack upon the rebs, on the Little Chicamauga at Ringgold, Georgia, and on Taylor's Ridge, and they fought desperately. Our brigade marched right up in front of their artillery, which they had planted in the gap between the mountains. Here the Thirteenth Illinois was stationed, and they stuck to the gap, fighting heroically, but were cut up badly, while my regiment, or rather the Fourth Iowa, of which I was a member, climbed up the ridge. We could injure the enemy but little for they would lie down on the top of the ridge, which was a circle in form; they had a crossfire upon us. It was a very bad place and we became much demoralized, when the Ninth Iowa came to our relief upon the right. We cheered and rushed forward with fixed bayonets, reaching for them, when the rebels fell back, and that vexed us very much, for as soon as were on equal footing with them they ran. We were so near them that the dead on both sides would fall in piles together, but they soon fled, and being so fleet of foot we followed them but a short distance, and weary, but cheerful, we turned our attention to caring for our fallen comrades. The Union losses in this battle, including the killed, wounded and missing, were reported to be about four thousand. More than six thousand rebel prisoners, not including the wounded, were here captured, besides forty-two pieces of artillery and many thousand small arms, and a large train. The loss to the rebels was not known. When the rebs fell back upon Taylor's Ridge in dismay they left their corn meal, sorghum and other supplies. We gathered them up. I ran for a sack of meal, which I got. C. E. Tibbles got some sorghum, so by and by we had something to eat.

November 28th, in camp on Little Chicamauga, near Ringgold in Georgia. Rained all day, being very disagreeable. Next day we moved our camp up in the timber. It was very cold and we were without tents or blankets, and nothing much to eat, as we had been cut off from our supply wagons so long, and marching and fighting all the time, and it being so cold that there was great suffering among the soldiers. On the 30th, C. E. Tibbles and I went out to see if could not find something to eat, but we had to return to camp with only one chicken.

CHAPTER VI.

Across the Tennessee—Barefoot Soldiers—Clayville, Alabama, Warned by Southern Sweethearts—Captured.

DECEMBER 7, 1863. We marched back near Chatta. nooga in Tennessee. Here we went into camp near the Georgia line. From this place we marched through Chattanooga and crossed the Tennessee river twice upon our pontoon bridges. Finally we arrived at Bridgeport, Alabama, where we remained several days in camp. Upon this march we were without tents or blankets. In fact we had nothing to shelter us from the inclement weather, and the only beds were branches of trees, when we could get them, or the cold, wet ground. We were nearly barefooted. After we were in camp here we drew our pay. I received $182, of which I sent $160 home. This would have been a good place to camp in dry weather, but during our stay it was very wet weather. It seemed we must be always on the move, so in a few days we were again ordered to march, so we proceeded to Stevenson, Alabama. Here we enjoyed a Christmas breakfast, which we received in trade for a pig which we had bagged that morning. We fell into line early and marched eight miles that day, which brought us to Scottsborough. We continued to march daily, making very little progress, owing to the bad roads and inclement weather. This region is subject to very sudden changes in temperature, which affect a northern man more than the steady cold of the north. We had rain, sleet, snow and mud in unstinted quantity.

January 1, 1864. At this place we had the coldest weather

of the winter. All this day I remained in camp and fed the fire with rails.

January 2, 1864. We moved our camp south to Woodville, a dryer and more desirable spot. Here we stayed some time. I went to the country several times to get a change of food, and paid fifty cents a meal.

There was considerable excitement in our camp at this time about re-enlisting as veterans, as our time was almost served out. A number of us who did not re-enlist were detached to Clayville, Alabama, to guard this little town from a large body of rebels. There was only about forty of us. Our boys used to go to see the confederate girls in town, which enraged the rebel soldiers who were on the opposite side of the Tennessee river upon which the town was located. We would go down to the river bank and tell the rebels on the opposite bank how we were courting the girls in town. This would make them so mad they would blaze away at us across the river. Our little force were in a very dangerous position here, but we were not at all alarmed, and the boys played the cavalier to the southern girls, and finally some of them were married to girls of this place. About this time our captain went home on a furlough, and a strange lieutenant was placed in command, who was a very incompetent man. His first act was to remove the guard from the river. The men expostulated with him, stating they would rather stand guard than to give the rebs a chance to surprise us. We were also told by our rebel girls that we would be surprised and all be killed if we were not on our guard. And so it proved to be; after this worthless officer had withdrawn the guards from the river we were at the mercy of our foes. We were only forty strong and slept in some shanties erected for barracks.

One night we were awakened by loud knocks upon our doors, which were immediately thrown open and volley after volley of small arms discharged into our rooms. As soon as we were dressed we returned the fire with effect, but were forced to surrender by the overwhelming numbers of the confederates. If we could have formed in company they would not have captured us so easily, if at all. It would have been better to have died then and there than to have suffered the way we did later on, while in their hands. I always thought it was wrong to send so small a force so far away from assistance in the vicinity of so large a body of rebels.

After our surrender we were stripped of everything of value. I had $65, which they took; also my best clothes, and my boots. Some of the boys were stripped nearly naked; some were the recipients of old shoes, but twelve were left barefooted. George B. Davis had some money in a belt which escaped the notice of our captors, which he magnanimously divided between us when we reached our destination, which proved to be Andersonville prison. We were crossed over the river that night, and on the morning of January 15th, we were started on our way to Rome, Georgia.

CHAPTER VII.

Man's Inhumanity to Man—Andersonville Prison Pen—Scenes and Events.

DEAR reader, I wish I could describe the place to which we were going, but no tongue can tell, no pen do justice to the horrors of Andersonville slaughter pen.

As before stated, we were left nearly naked; the weather was very cold—which was sufficient of itself to produce disease in healthy men, well clothed and well fed, who would have to undergo the treatment we did. We were given a very small ration of corn meal, and were informed we could have just fifteen minutes in which to cook it. But not being furnished with any cooking utensils we could do nothing with it. Some of our boys tried to eat it and others threw it away. Under these conditions we took up our march for Andersonville. We were marched twenty-five miles, when we stopped for the night in an old house. We had no fire; neither supper nor breakfast. This day we accomplished thirty miles. This night they gave us one pound of corn meal and eight ounces of bacon each, which was to last us two days. The next day as the sun began painting the eastern sky we commenced a thirty-five mile walk. That night as the guards slept, one of our boys awakened the rest of us, when we attempted to make our escape; but we found our legs were so swollen and stiff that we could scarcely stand, much less walk far enough to escape. So one of our boys called to the guard to awaken, or they might be found and put under arrest.

The next morning we found that snow had fallen two

inches deep. The suffering of those who were bare-footed cannot be described. With our feet already bleeding and mangled from coming in contact with rough surfaces, and the skin actually worn out, we were again forced to march. While we were stopping a few minutes, C. E. Tibbles, who had only a few rags tied around his feet, noticing one of our party whose feet were more mangled than the rest, told him to ask the guard to take him to a house near by and ask for some rags to tie about his feet, which he did. The woman— if it is proper to call her a woman—cursed him, called him an abolitionist, and said she would scald him if he did not get out of her house. We marched on. I am sure we could have been tracked by the blood left on the snow the last two days. About dark of this day we reached Rome. We were marched up the main street to a large three-story brick house. This house was filled with prisoners—I believe all of them suspects and deserters from the rebel army. When they saw us they called out: "Hang them! Bring them up, we will snatch them bald!" But when we were ushered into the room with these men, and our guards had gone, we found they were our friends. It can easily be understood why they threatened us in the presence of the guards. When we were alone, they shook hands with us, and showed the deepest feeling for our distress. They gave us their rations, divided their tobacco with us, and made us as comfortable as possible. They received with eagerness our information regarding our lines, and how they could reach them if they had a chance to run for it.

The next morning we were put on the cars and conveyed to Atlanta. Here we were kept in a pen for ten days, with shelter for only a part of us. For rations, we drew one pound of

meal and three-quarters of a pound of spoiled beef per man.
To add to the discomfort of our situation, the snow fell to the
depth of about four inches while we were in this pen, and our
feet were cut, swollen and ready to burst from our long march
over ice and snow bare-footed. Such, dear reader, was the
suffering of our men, that out of twelve who were bare-foot
at this time, only two were alive three months later, viz: C.
E. Tibbles and myself.

In this condition we were taken to Andersonville by rail;
the night we arrived was dark and rainy; when once inside
the walls, and our eyes became accustomed to the lights and
shadows of the place, we could see men sitting in groups in
all directions, small blue flames issued from the ground, which
we soon learned were from the resinous roots of pine stumps
which the prisoners had fired to warm by, and the roots had
burned deep into the sandy soil, and sent forth smoke continually.

Some of our boys remarked: " See those poor starved
negroes; it is shameful to treat them so." But when morning came, we found that they were not negroes, but some of
our own brave boys, whom starvation and exposure had
reduced to skeletons, and blackened by smoke and filth, had
the color of negroes.

Next morning I looked over our pen, and found it to be
about fourteen acres in extent, three acres of which was
swamp.   There was not a tent or even a board to shelter the
sick and dying, the violent storms, the merciless heat of the
sun above, the millions of crawling maggots which literally
covered every inch of ground, and other vermin which could
easily be discovered by putting the foot upon the ground for
a few moments and then examining it.   There was no place

for a man to lie down, and I did not lie down the first night.
As before stated, out of twelve bare-foot prisoners of our
squad, after two months but two were living, viz: C. E.
Tibbles and myself.

The mode of death of these ten prisoners was of the same
character, indicating death from Bright's disease of the kid-
neys. Extensive dropsy of the feet and legs would come on,
eventually the feet would burst; but several died before this
occurred. At night the sand was cold, during the day it was
hot. Our bed was upon the naked earth, and our covering no
less than the blue canopy of the starry-decked heavens. When
we first came to this prison there were only about six thousand prisoners, but afterwards they sent all their prisoners to
this place, until there were so many that we could not all lie
down at one time. We were without clothing, except when
some prisoner was fortunate enough to steal a meal sack, with
which he would endeavor to cover himself from the heat of
the day and the chill of the night. So numerous were the
sick and dying that the scarcely less feeble and starving companions could do nothing to render them assistance. So
numerous were the cries for assistance, that should a well man
attempt to pass from one side to the other of our prison, and
stop to assist each one who implored him piteously for assistance to rise, or for a drink of water, he would not make the
journey in a week. I am witness to the fact, that many
young men in good health, whose hair was black as the raven,
did, in twenty-four hours, become raving maniacs,—whose
hair became as white as the driven snow before the third day's
imprisonment. The food allowed each prisoner daily was one
pint of corn meal and four ounces of meat. The meat was
not such as would tempt the appetite of any but starving men.

This quantity was insufficient, so we were always hungry. It was the universal testimony of the prisoners that whenever they went to sleep, they would dream of something to eat. We would constantly dream of eating, and as certainly awaken as we were about to taste the food. I presume our anxiety to taste the food would awaken us.

Rain had its benefits as well as its disadvantages,—when it rained, the stream that ran through the pen would be purified to some extent; at the same time, every hard rain actually drowned many of our poor boys; many of them too weak to help themselves, would be strangled to death by the rain striking them in the face. One night when we had a particularly severe storm, more than two hundred perished in this way. And yet there are men to-day who cry, "down with the bloody shirt." You must not say anything to hurt the feelings of the rebel or his copper-colored accomplices of the north, "For Brutus is an honorable man."

It was some time in April,—we were not dying off fast enough to suit the Southern Confederacy,—so one morning we were called up in line and "vaccinated" with a deadly virus, which in all probability was poison taken from the decaying corpses, for the material caused symptoms identical with those which follow dissecting wounds. A lot of boys were sent in to act as surgeons; these boys would vaccinate one day, and in a few days would take all the arms off at the shoulders, of those who did not die from the vaccination.

One of our boys who was detailed to bury the dead, said that one day he would receive a great many arms to bury, and the next day he would get the same number of armless bodies.

Many of our boys suspected they were being poisoned, and

would find some way to cut out the part where the poison was inserted, and thereby saved their lives. C. E. Tibbles, George N. Tibbles and myself, for several months after making our escape from prison, were afflicted with dreadful sores; we were attended by the best of physicians. I escaped vaccination, having had the small-pox previous to my admission. But after I left Andersonville I suffered from "scurvy" and blood poisoning, and diseases of the lungs, which usually resulted in all those cases where a man was confined long enough, but lived to get out.

These poor fellows would frequently have large ulcers form under the arms, which would usually result in sloughing of the flesh covering the sides. This threw open the way to vermin, which soon found its way beneath the surface, and ended the victim's life by attacking the vital organs; to use a homely expression, they were eaten up alive. About one hundred and twenty dead were carried out and laid by the gate each morning. The appearance of these bodies was too shocking to be described in a book of this kind.

CHAPTER VIII.

Providence Springs—Trial of Mosby's Gang—Death Warrant Signed
by Abraham Lincoln—Attempts to Escape.

IT is true that in the Andersonville prison, during the
month of August, at a time when the water in the
branch had become scarce and foul and the captive
Unionists were dying by hundreds for want of pure water; it
is undoubtedly a fact, and whether it was a "special providence" or not, as most, if not all, of those wretched prisoners
believed, it served all the purposes of one. Of the origin of
this spring: during the month of August, 1864, the water in
the branch was indescribably bad. Before the stream entered
the stockade, it was rendered too filthy for any use by the
contaminations from the camp of the rebel soldiers, situated
above the prison. Immediately upon entering the stockade,
its pollution became terrible; the oozy seep at the bottom of
the hillside drained directly into it, all the filth from a popu-
lation of thirty-three thousand. Imagine the condition of an
open sewer through the heart of a city of that many people,
and receiving all the offensive products of so dense a popula-
tion into a shallow, sluggish stream, a yard wide and five
inches deep, heated by the burning rays of the sun at the
thirty-second parallel of latitude. At this awful extremity,
what was the astonishment and gratitude of the camp one
morning, when it was discovered that during the night a
large, bold spring had burst out upon the north side, about
midway between the branch and the summit of the hill, and
was pouring out a grateful flood of pure, cold water, in an

apparently inexhaustive quantity. This was the morning of August 13, 1864. The overjoyed Union prisoners christened it "Providence Springs."

Andersonville prison contained prisoners of almost every race. I noticed Indians, Chinese, Germans, Swedes, Englishmen and Negroes. There were surgeons, ministers, artists, mechanics and musicians. The rebels were anxious to get the mechanics to work for them, for which they gave an extra amount of food, of better quality, and furnished them shelter. But those who accepted of these offers were marked by us, and upon their return to prison we shaved one side of their heads, this was always done as a punishment for assisting our enemies. Our physicians were generally detached to assist as hospital stewards, where they did good work for our poor boys. There was a fellow known as Jim Malloy, who was a great sleight of hand performer; he had three assistants. It seemed that bolts and bars would not hold him. One night Jim and his three assistants were fastened to an iron bar by means of clevices. Malloy was quite a ventriloquist, and during the night the ignorant guard who stood over them, was startled by a solemn voice from the clouds, warning him of the vengeance to come upon the rebels for their cruelty to the Union prisoners, and while the guard stood trembling, behold the bars fell from their limbs, and they made their escape without hindrance.

Jim Malloy was supposed to be a spy; he escaped ten or twelve times, but was always recaptured. I think he always made his way to our lines and reported, when he would allow himself to be retaken.

There was a man in the prison named Mosby; he was first a bounty jumper, but afterwards raised a company of one hundred men and bushwacked—first on one side and then on the other. Finally he offered himself and men to Mosby on the Potomac. But contrary to his expectations, he was taken with all his men, and sent to Andersonville. Here he and his band formed themselves into a raiding, robbing gang of thieves and murderers. They would knock down the weak and the sick and take their rations from them; also anything else they had which they themselves wanted. Prisoners knocked down by this gang usually died of their wounds and sometimes were killed outright. Finally the rest of the prisoners associated together for mutual protection. We arrested him and his gang, and got permission from General Winder to try them for their lives. We chose a judge and jury—several lawyers volunteered for the prosecution; Mosby had some money, and hired the best counsel in the camp for his defense. Each man was tried separately. The court was in session several weeks. The jury found six guilty, and the judge sentenced them to be hung until dead. The papers were then sent to Washington, and came back signed by Abraham Lincoln. The day of execution came, and they were hung. The pleading was as good as was ever heard in a trial of this kind. The rebel officers and privates would come and listen for hours to the speeches, and examination of witnesses. General Winder was present one whole day, and seemed to have his curiosity aroused by the legal lore displayed by Uncle Sam's private soldiers.

The weather now became intensely hot, and as we had no hats, and no shelter from the direct rays of the sun, we were burned by the heat and the reflection from the sand until the skin would blister and form scabs over our faces, hands and feet; the pain of these burns was hard to bear; it resembled the pain felt upon being burned by hot iron. The wall of our prison was made of hewn logs, set in the ground six feet, and rising above the surface twenty feet; this shut off all the air from us, and acted as a barrier to any breezes that might come that way and blow off some of the offensive odors. The air we breathed and the water we drank were doing their work. An army of fresh, healthy prisoners would be brought in, and in a few days they would begin to look like the leaves in fall after the frost has touched them; in a few more days they would begin to disappear; the lines of dead lying just outside the stockade every morning would tell the sad story. The rebel doctors claimed, with evident satisfaction, that they were killing more men than Lee's whole army, and this was true. But was this not a cowardly, inhuman depravity? Such depravity as this belongs only to the South; no Northern soldiers could turn themselves into such inhuman fiends.

A platform ran around the stockade on the outside for the guards to walk upon, which placed them head and shoulders above the stockade. The dead-line was twenty feet from the wall, and the poor wretch who unwittingly came too near this line, was shot down with as much deliberation and heartlessness as one would shoot at a target. Very often when a prisoner would attempt to cross the branch, the guard would shoot him, and the amber-colored stream would blush again with loyal blood, and another rebel soldier get a furlough for taking the life of a Yankee.

We were constantly making tunnels; almost every night some of us would get out, only to be caught by bloodhounds and then punished. We would use a piece of tin canteen to dig with; the dirt we would throw around where we slept, to make believe we were fixing a place to sleep.

We came near all getting out one day; we had organized into regiments and divisions; officers were elected; we all had clubs. We had worked until one whole side of the prison was ready to fall; we intended to charge the battery the first thing, but when we were about ready to make a break, we found that one of our soldiers had divulged our plans. The traitor was taken out of prison, and that saved his life, for we would have killed him if we could have found him. One of our boys said that he knew the traitor, and that he would kill him if he ever saw him, if it was twenty years after, should he live to get out himself. After this the rebels stopped our rations one day and had all the earth filled in again.

CHAPTER IX.

Many Plans for Escape—Negroes' Singing—News from Atlanta—Rate of Deaths, one every Eleven Minutes.

THE prisoners were constantly devising every plan for escape. There was a company of about thirty-five laid a plan for escaping by drawing themselves up with a rope made out of rags strong enough to bear the weight of a skeleton. But like hundreds of others they were caught in the act of getting out, while others were chased and caught and torn by the thirsty blood-hounds. Some were even torn to pieces, but as this party was progressing nicely, as they thought, about fifteen had reached the summit of the stockade, and got on the outside, when the voice of a rebel guard rang out, "Halt, there, you d—— Yank." That was enough, the game was up. They were discovered, and the remaining twenty left that locality with all the speed in their power, getting away just in time to escape a volley, which a squad of guards, posted in the lookouts' poured upon the spot where they had been standing.

The next morning the fifteen who had got over the stockade were brought in, each chained to a sixty-four pound ball. This happened before they got to the dead-line. Their story was that one of the prisoners, who had become cognizant of their scheme, had sought to obtain favor at the rebels' hands by betraying them. The rebels stationed a squad at the crossing place, and as each man dropped down from the stockade he was caught by the shoulder and the muzzle of a revolver thrust into his face. It was expected that the guards in the sentry boxes would do such execution among those that were still inside, as would be a warning to others who should try to escape. They were defeated in this, for the prisoners scattered and fled from that place, and the man that divulged the plan was rewarded with a detail into the commissory department where he fed and fattened like a rat that had secured undisturbed homestead rights in the center of a cheese. When the miserable remnant of us were leaving Andersonville months afterward, he could be seen round and sleek and well-clothed, lounging leisurely in the door of a rebel tent. He was one of those milk and water men, such as we always have among us. They are no good. They cannot be trusted under any circumstances.

One time some traitor reported a tunnel when there was none, and the old captain stopped the rations of the entire prison till we would tell them where the tunnel was. In order to save the prisoners, two poor, starved wretches volunteered to start a tunnel, and when they got it started they went to Wirze and told him that they were the men that had started the tunnel, and the prisoners drew rations again. But alas, these two poor wretches were taken and tied up by the thumbs, and when they were cut down, they both fell to the ground. One of them finally got on his feet, but the other one expired. See what suffering one villainous traitor can cause.

These are the class of men that banded themselves together as raiders to rob the sick and dying. One day my comrade, C. E. Tibbles traded with the guard and got a small box of tobacco for which he paid five dollars in greenbacks worth fifty dollars in confederate money. He intended to trade part of his tobacco for corn meal or something else to eat, and one of those raiders came to him. However, Tibbles did not know it was a raider, and the raider told him he would trade him meal for tobacco, and asked him to go with him up where the meal was. Tibbles followed him until he got in the midst of the raider gang, and they took the tobacco and divided it among themselves and told Tibbles he had better get away, and Tibbles took them at their word and went away, for he had heard of them, but had never had a racket with them and did not desire one. But he came on and told how they had treated him, and it enraged us against the raiders, and our sergeant, W. W. Crandall, said, "by Him that liveth, we will have that tobacco or blood."

We were soon armed with clubs, which had been prepared before for their benefit.

Crandall marched his men up to the man that got the tobacco and demanded it, and he remarked: "Here is where you get it," and grabbed a club and gave the signal for fight, and in less than three minutes there were seventy-five raiders on the spot armed with clubs. The fight opened at once, but we soon found that we had undertaken more than we could accomplish, as they outnumbered us six to one. They rushed around us with a hop as though they were going to have some fun, but we made it hot for them for a short time, that is, until we could get away. Our clubs were about four feet in length and about the right heft to handle well, and we plied them right and left until we had wounded fifteen, and one mortally.

Every man in our squad got wounded but none mortally. We were always on the lookout after that, and never let them get the advantage of us again.

They attempted to make a raid on us one night about mid-

night, but we were on guard and we soon repulsed them and
drove them from our camp.   They were continually harrass-
ing the prisoners, and kept them in constant dread.

We were much interested in the negroes' singing.

They wove in a great deal of their peculiar, wild, mournful
music, according to the character of their labor.   They
seemed to sing the music for the music's sake alone, and seemed
heedless of the fitness of the accompanying words.   One middle aged man, with a powerful, mellow, clear voice, was the
musical leader of the party; he never seemed to bother himself about air, notes or words, but impressed all as he went
along; and he sang as the spirit moved him.   He would suddenly break out with,

"Oh he's gone up dah, nevah to come back again."

at this every darkey, within hearing, would break out, in ad-
mirable consonance with the pitch, air and time started by
the leader, "o-o-o-o-o-o-o-o-o-o-o!"   Then would ring out from
the leader as from the throbbing lips of a silver trumpet,

"Lord bless him soul! I done hope he is happy now!"

and the two hundred would chant back "o-o-o-o-o-o-o-o-o-o-o!"
and so on for hours.   They never seemed to weary of singing
and we certainly did not of listening to them.   The absolute
independence of the manner and tune and sentiment, gave
them freedom to wander through camp with harmonic effect,
as spontaneous and changeful as the song of a bird.

I have sat evening after evening, with some comrade and
listened to them sing and chant, long after the shadows of
night had fallen upon the hillside.

THE NEGRO SINGING AT NIGHT.

And the voice of his devotion
Filled my soul with strong emotion;
For its tones by turns were glad,
Sweetly solemn, wildly sad.

Paul and Silas, in their prison,
Sang of Christ, the Lord arisen,
And an earthquake's arm of might
Broke their dungeon gates at night.

But, alas what holy angel
Brings the slave this glad evangel?
And what earthquake's arm of might,
Breaks his prison gates at night?

The rebs tried every plan to discourage us, but that was of
no use to attempt such a thing, for we would not believe
them, and we well knew our condition could not be worse.
When Sherman was fighting at Atlanta we could get but little news only through the rebel papers, but they pretended all
the time that Sherman's defeat was certain.

Next came news that Sherman had raised the seige and fallen back at the Chattahoohee, and we felt something of the
bitterness of despair for several days.

Therefore we heard nothing, though the hot, close summer
air seemed intense with a war storm about to burst, even as
nature heralds in the same way a concentration of the mighty
force of the elements for the grand crash of the thunder-
storm. We waited with intense expectancy for the decision
of the fates; whether final victory or defeat should end the
long and arduous campaign. At night the guards in the
perches around the stockade called out every half hour, so as
to show the officers that they were awake and attending to

4

their duty. The form for this ran thus: "Post number 1; half-past eight o'clock, and a-l-l'-s w-e-l-l!" Post No. 2 repeated this cry, and so it went around.

One evening when our anxiety as to Atlanta was wrought to the highest pitch, one of the guards sang out. "Post No. 4; half past eight o'clock—and Atlanta's-gone-to-h——l!"

The heart of every man within hearing leaped upward. We looked toward each other almost speechless with glad surprise, and then cried out: "Did you hear that." The next instant a ringing cheer burst out spontaneously from the throats and hearts of men in the first ecstatic moments of victory—a cheer to which our sad hearts and enfeebled lungs had long been strangers. It was the genuine, honest, manly northern cheer, not like the rebel yell. But the shout was taken up all over the prison, even those who had not heard the guard understood that it meant Atlanta was ours, and fairly won.

We had a time of rejoicing; we assembled together in different parts of the stockade and sung patriotic songs and made speeches, and there was a general awakening in camp.

It set our thin blood to bounding, and made us remember that we were Union soldiers, with higher hopes than that of starving and dying in Andersonville. The rebels became excited lest our exhaltation of spirit would lead to an assault upon the stockade. They came out with arms and remained so until the enthusiasm became less demonstrative. The rebels would try to make us think we would soon be exchanged, which would cause some excitement, but all hope would soon vanish, and the prisoners would exclaim: "No exchange for us until we are exchanged to that eternal God's country where

Sickness and sorrow, pain and death,
Are felt and feared no more.

The wish for fame is faith in holy things
That soothe the life, and shall outlive the tomb.—
A reverent listening for some angel wings
That come above the gloom.

The weather is now intensely hot and thousands of our brave comrades have already descended into an untimely grave within the last few months, and I believe their death was caused by the filthy camp, and the want of good food and water, proper medicine, and the breeding of lice on our poor frames. I could see no alternative but we would all very soon share the same untimely grave of our comrades. Solemnity seemed to rest on the entire camp. Must this thing go on? Is there no help? I had a great yearning to be up and doing something to turn these golden hours to good, pressed into heart and brain awakening to energetic life. But this ambition had fled from thousands of our brave comrades.

The starving and the heat and the cruel rains sapped away their stamina, and they could not recover it with the innutritious diet of a little coarse meal and an occasional scrap of poor meat. Quick consumption, bronchitis, pneumonia, low fever, scurvy and diarrhœa seized upon these ready victims for their ravages, and bore them off by the hundreds. The appearance of the dead was indescribable. The unclosed eyes shone with a stony glitter, the lips and nostrils were distorted with pain and hunger. The dirty, grimed skin drawn tensely over the bones, and the whole frame with the long, matted hair and beard. As I have stated before, you could not tell a dead man from the living when they were still, if it was not for the breathing millions of lice swarming over the wasted limbs, face and eyes. These verminous pests had become so numerous, as we had no change of clothing, and no facilities for boiling even what we had. The best that any of us could do was to keep the number reduced so they would would not sap our blood at once. When a man became so sick or poor as to be unable to help himself, he soon passed out. The number of the lice would increase to multiplied millions. I have heard prisoners say that they had seen a gallon of lice on one dead man at one time.

No doubt but the biting of these horrible insects shortened the lives of those who died. I wish to impress this on your mind; think, for a moment, if you were as stout as Henan, and you were cast in an open pen, such as I have described; could a man live there? No. As the weather grew warmer and the number in the prison increased, the lice became more unendurable; they even filled the sand; and they would crawl upon us like streams of ants running up a tree. I thought it must be something like Egypt was when the Lord sent the third plague.

"And the Lord said unto Moses say unto Aaron stretch out thy rod, and smite the dirt of the land, that it may become lice through all the land of Egypt. And they did so; for Aaron stretched out his hand with his rod, and smote the dust of the earth, and it became lice, and all the dust of the land became lice throughout all the land of Egypt."

We could have gone through a sharp campaign, lasting thirty days, and not lose so great a number of men as died in Andersonville in the same length of time. A make shift of a hospital was established inside the stockade. A small portion of ground was divided from the rest of the prison by a railing, and a few tent flies were stretched. And in those they used pine boughs for beds. If a man was so sick that he could not walk about and was taken in this hospital it was sure death, and almost sudden. This was the sort of hospital we had in Andersonville for our sick and dying comrades. What was needed to bring about health was clean clothing, nutritious food, shelter and freedom from the tortures of the lice and from the sight of the horrors of such a prison. And the sick was fed the same coarse corn meal which hurried the poor wretch into eternity. They wore and slept in the same vermin-infested clothing, and there could be but one result. The establishment of the hospital was unfortunate for the prisoners. The ground required for it compelled a general reduction of the space we all occupied, for some who had shanties built with pine boughs were now compelled to tear them down and we were so crowded that we could scarcely all lie down at the same time.

The chief causes of the deaths were the scurvy and its effects, and bowel affections—chronic and acute diarrhœa and dysentary. The bowel affections appeared to have been due to the diet, the dejected state of the nervous system and moral and intellectual powers, and to the effluvia arising from the filth of the prison.

The great disease of scurvy seemed to be prevalent; this disease, without a doubt was also caused, to a great extent, in its origin and course, by the foul animal emanations. From the sameness of the food and from the action of the poisonous gases in the densely crowded and filthy stockade and hospital. The blood was altered in its condition even before the manifestation of actual disease.

The most men that ever died in Andersonville was one man every eleven minutes, except the night we had a severe rain storm when two hundred perished. The boys would put in a great deal of time killing lice and looking at their swollen legs and feet and working with their sore arms, etc., etc.

One day my comrade, C. E. Tibbles, asked a poor fellow what our feet and legs looked like? He replied I give it up. Charley replied, they look like an Irish potato with two goose quills sticking in it.

We did everything we could to keep the boys roused up as we well knew that when despondency set in upon them that death was the inevitable result.

CHAPTER X.

Terrible Suffering—Trying to Effect an Exchange—A Novel way of Concealing Escaped Prisoners—Escape of Three—Overtaken by Blood Hounds and Recaptured—The Rebels try to Enlist the Prisoners of Andersonville into the Rebel Army.

> "On Fame's eternal camping ground
>   Their silent tents are spread,
> While Glory guards with solemn round,
>   The bivouac of the dead."

DEAR reader, although it is now more than twenty years ago, I cannot recur to these horrors without gloomy feelings; I have seen hundreds of poor men sitting about the prison, with their legs buried in the sand, to keep them from bursting, they were so swollen with the scurvy; and I have often seen poor, starved skeletons pick up old dry bones from the sand and boil them to make soup. Reader it is worse to experience these suffering than to read of them. I have experienced all that I have written, and more than I can ever tell, and therefore I take no man's word for it. I will here relate an instance portraying the undying patriotism of those suffering prisoners. We held a meeting while at Andersonville, by permission of the rebel authorities, and there appointed five delegates to go to Washington to see if they could not effect an exchange. The terms upon which the rebels agreed to exchange where these: "The union Government was to release all their prisoners held by the North, and the rebels to release all held by them, the excess held by the Union army to be paroled." When those terms were made known to the

prisoners, it was upon the day appointed by the delegates to
start, and when they started, the prisoners called after them
as long as they could make them hear, "Tell old Abe never
to back down for us, we can stand it until Sherman comes,
for we would rather die than back down to rebs," etc., etc.
I have known some of the prisoners to get paints of the guards
and make ten-dollar greenback bills and trade them to the rebs
for good money or something to eat—one dollar in greenbacks
being worth ten dollars in Confederate money—and many
other little things they resorted to, which might be tiresome
to the reader.

It finally became necessary to have a large force of men
to bury the dead, as those who were already detailed were far
behind in the interment of the bodies, and the rebs got afraid
that they would create a pestilence in their own camps;
another detail was therefore made, and I managed to get myself and some of my comrades placed upon it. As it was impossible for a man to work on the rations issued in the prison,
the grave-diggers were allowed double rations. We were
placed upon their parole and allowed to go anywhere within
a mile of their grave-yard. The arms of the working parties
soon became very sore from the eff cts of the foul vaccination,
but rather than go back into the pestilential stockade they
would swing the pick with one arm; even when so sick we
could not eat what little rations we received. Some of the prisoners were continually breaking out of the stockade and for a
long time the diggers succeeded in effectually concealing them
in rather a novel way: there was always a long line of dead
bodies awaiting burial, and when a prisoner came to us, we
would shove some of the dead bodies slightly apart and put
the escaped and living skeleton between them, and when his

eyes were closed he could not be distinguished from the dead. The rebels put all of us in the stockade to make us tell where we hid those who had escaped, but no one ever divulged it. So when night came on we would give the escaped prisoners our rations and start them on their way. One day a rebel officer, a lieutenant, came to us and proposed for us to break our parole and run away to our lines with him, as he knew the country, and we must also insure him good treatment when once within our lines; but after taking the matter under consideration, we decided not to do it; this same lieutenant gave one of us a jacket and did all he could for us. Many of the diggers did escape, and finally the rebs released us from our parole and placed a guard over us. Our conscience being now free, we began to meditate seriously upon an escape. An opportunity soon presented itself. The rebs had formed guard lines around the grave-yard; but covered wagons were used to bring dead bodies from the prison. Two of the diggers were placed in each wagon upon its return to the stockade, and the curtains being tied down, two of us would slip out while on the road on the first trip, and hid in the swamp near by until the next trip, when another comrade and a fellow-prisoner followed us, and we immediately took up our line of march for "*God's country.*" Our path lay for miles through a swamp, and at every step we would stick in the mire knee deep, except when we could step upon the roots of swamp brush. Sometimes one would stick fast, and the rest of us would pull him out as best we could by the aid of the swamp willows. Although weak and diseased, we toiled on all night long; the "North Star" and the " Big Dipper " were our guides.

C. E. Tibbles, George N. Tibbles and myself have gone

together all through the war, and were in prison together, and were now trying to make our escape from Andersonville together; but knew not how far we would get.

After traveling all night through the swamp and brush land, and crossing several fields, we were very tired, and sat down upon some fallen trees to rest for a few minutes; but had only got comfortably settled when we heard the baying of the hounds; we knew then that our enemies were close upon us; we darted into the dark forest and ran; we were very weak, but we ran some fifteen miles before we stopped. On and on came the deep-mouthed baying of the hounds, but it was difficult for them to make way through the swamp. The sounds became fainter, and seemed to die away in the distance. We now continued flight; we passed through hog pens, stock yards, and ran back and forth to destroy our trail; we also ran through deep sand, hoping when we pulled out our feet the sand would fill in and cover our scent. We urged our fast failing strength and pushed on until morning, when we found ourselves upon the border of a large plantation, and people moving about. We dare not cross for fear of discovering ourselves to the occupants of this place. So we laid ourselves down in a small piece of timber, hoping to escape notice until night should give us cover to move on. During the forenoon we saw some negroes and a white man coming directly towards our hiding place. We concealed ourselves as best we could. They came very near, and the white man said, pointing to a small tree. "Here, boys, this will do." The negroes soon cut the tree down, and the top of it fell upon the bushes beneath which we were hiding, but only served to hide us more completely from view. In a few hours we saw a negro approaching us again, upon his shoulder he bore an ax. He came up to within fifteen feet of us, and looked at us for some time. When C. E. Tibbles raised up and started towards him the negro raised his ax. We then told him that we were his friends, and charged him to tell no one that we were there. He said he would not, and left us. We changed our position a little, and cut each man a good stout club. We were making calculations upon crossing the river below Sherman's army that night, when we would be safe.

Just about sunset we were congratulating ourselves on having given the hounds the slip, when the distant baying sent a thrill of horror through us all. Andersonville was before us again, with all its dead and dying; our blood stood still. Nearer and near came the yelping of the hounds. We must do something. We ran from our hiding place and agreed if they pressed us too closely we would scatter, and every man take care of himself. We had not half cleared the field when the hounds were upon us,—what were we to do?—it was too late to scatter now. Perplexing as was our situation, we could not keep down a hearty laugh. The rebels had started with forty hounds, but ten had given out in the swamp. The hounds came up and attacked us savagely. We kept them from tearing us with our clubs. Here came the keepers on well jaded horses, for we had traveled over forty miles from late the evening before. We were now upon the fence, fighting the dogs off with our clubs. The brutal keepers ordered us to get down. We told them to call off their dogs and then we would. They said they were ordered to let the dogs tear us, at the same time drawing their revolvers. We told them to shoot, that we would as lief be shot as to return to Andersonville. One was about to shoot, but was reminded that if he shot and killed any of us, he would lose his one hundred dollars reward, which was always paid for capturing an escaped prisoner. Still it seemed we were to die at the hands of the men and thirty hounds, but we determined we would fight with our last breath.

> "For, how can a man die better,
> Than facing fearful odds
> For the ashes of his fathers
> And the temples of his gods."

As an instance of the patriotism of our soldiers, I wish here to cite a circumstance of prison life:

At one time the rebel leaders endeavored to enlist the prisoners in Andersonville into the rebel army. One day we were ordered to form into companies, with the proper officers of each company and division in their places, and to march outside the prison walls. We were very much excited—many thought we were to be exchanged. We could not divine what it was for, until we were regularly formed outside, when a rebel officer mounted a stump and began a speech to us. He informed us that the United States Government had left us to our fate; that McClelland and other Union generals had said that they could get along without us; that the Confederacy was sure to succeed; that the Northern people cared nothing about us, and would never try to rescue us. Then followed an appeal to us to no longer endure the prison pen, but to join the rebel army, and each of us should have a farm when the Union army was whipped. No sooner was he understood, than the sergeant of our division sprang out and shouted: *Attention, First Division!* This was repeated down the line by hundreds of other sergeants. He shouted: *First Division, About!* This was repeated by thousands, as one voice. Then he said: *Face!* Then by the thousands we all turned on our heels and came to order. *Forward, march!* We marched back into the pen, one division after another, and left the orator standing on the stump. Here we view another instance of the devotion of our boys in blue. The rebels were greatly provoked at the failure of their venture, and showed it by coming into our pen in armed squads on the pretense of looking for spades and shovels, and destroyed our shanties, stole our blankets, or anything else they wanted.

CHAPTER XI.

Return to Prison—Punishment—Confederate Government Knew of the Treatment at Andersonville—Jeff Davis Accessory to the Murder of Thirteen Thousand Prisoners of War.

"How sleep the brave, who sink to rest,
By all their country's wishes blest!
By fairy hands their knell is rung,
By forms unseen their dirge is sung,
Their honor comes—a pilgrim gray—
To bless the turf that wraps their clay;
And freedom shall a while repair,
To dwell a weeping hermit there."

HUNGRY and disheartened, we were marched back to our prison pen. We were marched fifteen miles the first night, which took nearly all night. We were furnished with no food on this trip. I shall not try to describe the sufferings and abuse we endured. Upon reaching the prison, we were immediately taken before Captain Wirze, at his headquarters. Directly in front of his headquarters he had erected a scaffold, upon which to hang some recaptured prisoners. As we marched up he raised his head, and looking us over, inquired: "Where is that Will Crandall? I gives five hundred tollars for that Will Crandall." Crandall was a prisoner who escaped the evening before we did; he was subsequently caught. We told him we knew nothing of Crandall. Then he turned his vicious, small eyes upon us and began to curse us, and said: "I makes a hell for you. You shall bury all the prisoners who die," meaning the forty of us,

and we were to work on half rations, and he said that he
would keep us in the stocks at night, and that we should stay
in the stocks thirty days after the other prisoners had gone
home. This was a hard sentence. The stocks would have
caused death in less than ten days, but the fear of death had
long departed, death on every hand had become so familiar
that he seemed a friend to the poor, wretched shadows that
we were. We did not, however, have to endure this long. I
wish to state what was meant by "stocks." Two planks
made to fit the neck, wrists and ankles, which were keyed up
tight; with the apparatus adjusted, a man could not sit down
nor lie down. Another mode of punishment should be described here. It consisted of chaining ten or fifteen men together, with a twenty-four pound cast ball attached to each
man, in the center was a cast ball of one hundred and sixty
pounds, to which each man was chained. This also soon
caused death.

About 9 A. M. we were sent to dig graves, with a guard of
forty men placed over us. We dug trenches about one hundred and sixty feet long and three feet deep, and at the bottom of this we dug a vault of one foot in depth. Jake Hela-
maker, of Ohio, and myself split slabs and placed one over
each of our dead. We also, as far as could be done, placed a
board with regiment, company and name. The reader is well
aware that it is no small task to bury one hundred and twenty
men each day; that was about the number carried out every
morning. So badly would they decompose during the interval
between death and burial that often we found, when we attempted to lift them, that the skin slipped from the flesh, and
often the flesh cleared from the bone, for most of the poor fellows were suffering from scurvy. The flesh of these bodies

was soft and very black by the time it reached the grave diggers. Here comes a government wagon piled full of our brave boys; thrown into the wagon like a lot of dead swine, to be as rudely thrown out again on their arrival at the burial ground.

We were so starved now in the pen that we were glad to catch mice, bugs, grasshoppers, crickets, or anything that could be eaten, and woe to the unfortunate dog or cat that ventured within our reach; nothing is too bad for starving men to eat. Murder is tame when compared to the acts of these Southern fiends. I wish in the following pages to give a statement as evidence in support of what I have said regarding this prison, and the infamous purpose of the prison general commanding, General F. H. Winder, the commanding officer in charge of the post, some months after the close of war. Captain Henry Wirze, a subordinate, having immediate command of the prison, was arraigned before a military court in Washington for brutal treatment and unnecessary cruelty to his prisoners. The facts we have here stated were corroborated by many Union soldiers, summoned as witnesses, and he was found guilty of such base cruelty that he was sentenced and hung. C. E. Tibbles, one of our squad who had received such base treatment from Wirze, had the pleasure of giving his testimony against him, and of seeing his execution. But more valuable testimony, considering the source from which it emanated, was given by Colonel D. T. Chandler, formerly inspector general in the rebel service. The following is an extract from an official report from this officer, addressed to Colonel Chilton, at Richmond, under date of August 5, 1864:

"My duty requires me to respectfully recommend a change in the officer in command of the post, by putting in a substitute in Brigadier

General Winder's place, one who will unite both *energy* and *good judgment*, with some feeling of humanity and consideration for the welfare and comfort (as far as is consistent with their safe keeping) of the vast number of unfortunates placed under his control, some one who will not advocate deliberately, and in cold blood, the propriety of leaving them in their present condition, until their number has been sufficiently reduced by death to make the present arrangement suffice for their accommodation. Who will not consider it a matter of self-laudation—boasting that he has never been inside the stockade—a place the horror of which it is difficult to describe, and which is a disgrace to civilization, the condition of which he might (by the exercise of a little energy and judgment) even with the limited means at his command, have considerably improved."

Colonel Chandler, upon being called to the stand, verified the foregoing statement, or report, adding that he had nothing to retract, and further stated that during his inspection he had a conversation with General Winder, who seemed very indifferent to the wellfare of the prisoners, and was not disposed to do anything. He remonstrated with Winder as best he could. He spoke of the great mortality, and suggested that as the sickly season was coming on, the swamp should be drained, and better food furnished, and other sanitary measures adopted. But Winder replied to him that he thought it would be better to let one-half die, so they could take care of the remainder. Chandler's assistant, Major Hall, had previously reported that Winder had made a simple statement to him, and upon Chandler's remarking that he thought this incredible, Major Hall said Winder had repeated that expression to him several times.

So this certainly shows that the rebel government in Richmond was made officially cognizant of the barbarities committed at Andersonville, and of the condition of the prisoners

5

at Belle Isle, and had been so immediately under their eyes that ignorance could not possibly have been pleaded. The conclusion seemed inevitable that they deliberately approved of the measures adopted by the commanding officers at both places.

CHAPTER XII.

A Change of Prisons—Escape at Belle Isle—Living on Green Corn—The
Swamps—Blood Hounds—Despair in the Swamps.

> Press on! If once and twice thy feet
> Slip back and stumble, harder try;
> From him who never dreads to meet
> Danger and death, they're sure to fly.
> To coward ranks the bullet speeds,
> While on their breast who never quail,
> Gleams, guardian of chivalric deeds,
> Bright courage, like a coat of mail.

THE reader, no doubt, will be convinced by the foregoing
proof of the complicity of Davis and his cabinet in this
wholesale murder department of the Southern Confederacy.

We must now give our attention to grave-yard and prison,
where we were last seen digging graves for murdered comrades. We were not working here many days until we could
notice a degree of restlessness among the guards. We soon
learned that the rebels feared a raid from Sherman on Andersonville, which I often thought could have been accomplished.
So one day there came orders to send a part of the prisoners
to Florence, S. C. We were taken with others, and placed
upon the cars. We were informed that we were to be
exchanged, which was merely done to taunt us. Captain
Wirze came to us and said, "You —— ——, you think you
are going to get off, but I have sent orders for you to be placed
upon the same rations you enjoyed here. I will learn you
how to run away."

Tibbles and myself were on the lookout for a chance to escape; our sentence still hung over us; our two days' rations were exhausted; nine hundred men upon the train, and nothing to eat. Tibbles and myself had been fortunate enough to obtain some rice from the guards at Andersonville, having traded with them for a small supply before starting. This rice was all we had for two days, until we reached Florence, on the 16th of September, 1864. Here they took us off of our train and guarded us. Tibbles and I went all around and through the crowd of prisoners and tried to get them to make a dash upon our guards. I offered to take the gun from either of the guards, but the prisoners were so deeply discouraged that they would only laugh at us. Many of our boys thought we could never reach the Union line if we were turned loose. I, in common with others, thought it was life or death with us, and I determined I would not go inside the stockade at Florence.

G. N. Tibbles managed to slip out past the guards, got a woman to bake him a corn cake, and then came back inside the guard line, and three of us ate half of it, the rest was put away in our haversacks, to be used on our journey. For we determined to go through the lines and escape, or leave our dead bodies as a memento of our last attempt.

We had been fortunate enough to find a map. We studied it, and decided to strike for Newbern, N. C. We thought from looking over our map it must be about three hundred miles up the coast, and thought we could find enough raw corn in the fields to live on, and determined we would not ask for any thing to eat on this trip, or speak to any one, but pursue a northernly course and travel by night. But, great heavens! as we concluded our arrangements, they began to move us to the stockade. Something must be done. As we turned a curve in the road—the guards were a little too far apart—C. E. Tibbles, G. N. Tibbles and myself darted into the brush, ran a few yards into a strip of undergrowth, when we found the railroad in front and the wagon road in the rear. Many men were going to and from the prison. Here we dropped down and laid as flat on the leaves as we could. We laid here until near sunset, when a rebel came up within twenty feet of us, and looked directly at us a short time, he then turned and went away. So soon as he was out sight we sprang to our feet and ran across the railroad. By this time he was back to the place we had left with an armed guard to take us back.

We ran with all the speed we could, while shouts of the soldiers behind us to halt, the ping of the bullet as it struck over our heads, or tore through the thickets, only had the effect to increase our speed. On and on we ran, out into the dismal swamp. Here we began to breath easier, and about dark we fell in with another fugitive, who informed us that his name was Charles F. Davis. We now came to a field of corn, where we ate our fill, and gathered as much as we could, which we lived on almost altogether for the succeeding three or four days. We had a portion of the cake which the woman had baked for Tibbles, this delicacy we wished to save for future use, for "Coming events cast their shadows before." But we did eat a piece of cake about as large as a silver dollar each day.

We now came to the river called the Big Piney on the fourth day; this river we must cross; we feared the bridge, for it was likely to be guarded. While we were undecided what to do, we suddenly discovered a negro in the bush, within a few feet of us. The negro seeing we were all alarmed said, "Go on, massa; go on, God bless you." When we discovered that he was friendly, we eagerly inquired of him which way we had better go, and whether the bridge was guarded. He informed us that there was a guard of five hundred at the bridge, and death would be certain if we attempted to cross there. But he gave us directions by which we crossed the river in safety. Once across the river we looked for and found, our old friend, the "North Star," which has guided so many of our poor boys through swamp and canebrake to God's country.

Shortly after getting our bearing, we were greeted by the baying of hounds. Soon a whole pack of them came bounding, wide-mouthed upon us. We fought as only men know how to fight whose lives are at stake. We fought the dogs with clubs, and it was with great difficulty we beat them off. We would strike until we were ready to fall with exhaustion. A man living on raw corn does not develop very great strength, and it is a wonder how we could fight off these hounds in our weakened condition; but we did finally beat them off, and got away from them. We dared not build a fire for fear the smoke would attract attention, so we ate our corn raw. We determined never to grace another rebel prison. We were now traveling through a dense thicket or swamp, which was thickly grown with long green briars, which grew across the paths and open spaces through which we made our way, and tore our clothes, and lacerated our flesh as we hurried on in the darkness.

Morning came at last, and all day long we traveled through swamp, thicket and bog; bog, thicket and swamp. Now we could not see the stars, so thick and tall was the undergrowth, except we look directly up at the heavens through the chinks of the over-hanging growth of swamp brush and briars, so we concluded we would try the road. We decided to send one of our number on, as an advance guard, twenty steps ahead of the rest, and if our advance was fired upon it would give the rest some chance to escape without being seen. We traveled in this fashion for sixteen days and nights. Sometimes when it was too light to travel in the roads, and too dark to travel in the swamp, we would lie down and take a little sleep until the night grew darker, when we would return to the road. We only slept three nights out of the sixteen. The first two nights we did not lie down at all. One of these nights I felt we were going in the wrong direction, but the others would not listen to me; but when we saw the morning star we found we were going wrong, and then we changed our course northeast. On and on, there seemed no end to the swamps, and our sufferings; starving, weak and trembling, our courage and the hope of again seeing the land of the free and the home of the brave alone supported us in these, our last trials.

One night we came to water, it was a very dark night, and we followed along the shore until we came to what seemed to be a bridge; leading up to the bridge were steps, upon which we mounted and crossed on the slab-covered tressle, which seemed to be about thirty feet above the water; so dark was it we could not see the structure on which we walked—or rather felt our way. The farther end of this bridge seemed to end in the tree tops. We finally came to the shore in safety, although we had feared guards would be there to intercept us.

We were now about thirty miles from Wilmington, N. C., and the intervening country was very low and nearly all swamp.

These swamps are very desolate, and almost devoid of sunshine, the trees are covered with the clinging vines peculiar to this climate, which shut out the light of day. I believe there are bears and other wild animals capable of taking the life of man which live in these swamps. We where chased by a large grizzly bear one day for quite a distance but by careful watching we evaded him and escaped this dangerous foe. He followed us three miles.

We could not tell when we were nearing a rebel camp until we would see a rebel picket. One morning, just before daylight, we came to one and we all drew our clubs, and was in the act of killing him, when he spoke to us, and so friendly, too, that we passed on. He thought we were rebels, of course, going into camp, as what clothes we had on were of rebel uniform. But we concluded to go round the rebel camp this time. One evening about sunset we discovered a terrible storm arising, and we went to the road and traveled on, and in a short time we discovered a man run across the road from a barn, and in a moment the storm was dashing and raging furiously. We ran for the barn, and by this time the air was full of trash, limbs, lumber and streaks of lightning. The storm very nearly demolished the barn, but we remained unhurt. As soon as practicable we resumed our weary march onward. We soon approached a small village, it being just after dark, we passed on along through the streets. We could see the citizens in groups looking at us, and soon after we passed out of town, we perceived they had gathered together quite a company of men and were pursuing us; but we started on the Indian trot and were soon lost to their view in the deep forests filled with greenbriers, vines and brush, until it really looked impossible for anything to pen-etrate the swamp but wild beasts. So they soon gave up the chase not wishing to be torn by the briers, as we were compelled to be.

We traveled on and the next day as we had traveled through swamps, and had had no chance to get ourselves any corn to eat, we were getting very weak and faint; along in the afternoon we crossed a deep gulch on a small pole. It was with difficulty that we crossed at all, and as soon as we crossed we came out at a cross roads, and there stood a rebel picket guard. We turned instantly and ran across the pole without the least difficulty, we ran about forty rods and then crossed again and ran on and were soon away into a swampy desert, with blood hounds and rebels pursuing us. On we went a tearing through the long green briers. We could distinctly hear the blood hounds on our trail. We ran on and on until our strength was all exhausted, and our feet and legs torn and bleeding. Our pants were nearly all torn off of us, and we had had nothing to eat since the day before, and had traveled all night and ran nearly all day and could not get even raw corn to eat, nor no water. O! my pen refuses to portray our sufferings, bleeding and torn, starving and famishing. All hope of life had now vanished from us. We reeled and fainted and fell, and as we fell it was near a large mossy old stump. One of the party who had claimed that he did not believe the Bible when we were in prison, now whispered and said: "let us all pray our best." Now here we lay starving and dying and weeping like lost children; for we had suffered and toiled so much, and then to have to die there away in the swamps, be eaten up by wild beasts and our friends neven know what had become of us. A vision of mine that God had revealed to me before the war. Things had come to

pass just as it was pictured out to me then, and I fully believed at that time that it was a warning from God to me. It
deeply impressed my mind then and for sometime after, for
you know the blessed Bible teaches us that God warns his
people of danger and delivers those that put their trust in
him.

CHAPTER XIII.

Still Fleeing through Swamps—No Food for Thirty-eight Hours—Still
Pursued by Blood-hounds—A Rain brings Relief and Destroys their
Trail.

> Ask not the wanderers after our fate,
> Our being, birth or name;
> Enough that all have shared our state,
> And we are still the same.
>
> Green briers and thorns our life has torn,
> Still strives our souls within,
> While care, pain, and sorrow show,
> That we starved and perished in the swamps.

WHILE lying there in that swamp, I offered the prayer to
God that Peter offered when he was sinking in the
water, "Lord save or we perish." But I continued on
thusly, "but not my will, but *thine* be done." My faith in
God to save me was unwavering, though all other hopes had
failed. While we were yet lying there weeping and praying
in our hearts, for we never spoke a loud word for fifteen
days in all our conversation, we just whispered, our suffering
was intense. C. E. Tibbles remarked that "we had just as
well die here." But I replied, that "we had just as well die
walking along as lying here." But hark! Listen! we again
hear the bloodthirsty troop in pursuit of us. In an instant
we are on our feet, and each man took his own course
through the swamps like so many wild beasts fleeing from
the hunter. I never expected to see my comrades again in

this life. On and on we fled through the dense forest of green briers and swamp brush, when all at once we found ourselves come together in one squad again. In a short time a cloud passed over, and it rained quite a shower. It was now about 5 o'clock in the evening, and we licked the leaves for the water on them and hunted little cups, and got a little water out of them, and this was the first water we had had for twenty-four hours. That little shower gave us water and washed our tracks until the hounds could not track us, consequently they were compelled to give us up. We traveled on until dark with our legs bleeding and naked, they were so torn by the briers. It was now dark and we were all wet, running through the wet brush, and seemingly we were about the center of the swamp, and it was very wet and muddy, and we stuck sticks in the ground and sucked up some water. It was now so dark, and the briers, brush and vines were so thick we could not see to get through; as we could not see the north star, we could not tell the direction so we all lay down there in the wet and mud with our limbs on the wet ground. Here we lie shivering, starving skeletons; we had had no food for thirty-eight hours. I felt that no power could save us but the power of God.

And I felt that I did not care much only to live to tell my friends where I had been, and try to serve God. Now while we lay there piled up in that muddy swamp our sufferings were so great that I have no idea that we will ever suffer more or half so much the day of our death as we suffered that day and night. My mind was in heaven with my dear angel mother, that went up there when I was a small boy and then with my old father in Iowa. It seemed to me that I could feel a stream of love flitting from heaven to me and from me to my father in Iowa. My father afterwards told me, when I got home, that that night he could not sleep, that it was impressed on his mind that I was about to perish and he got up out of bed and asked God to save me. Every time he would lie down in bed that night the same whispering would come to him, until he got up and prayed three times. It seemed to me that I could feel the flitting of angel's wings hovering over me. I thought perhaps that angels had come to conduct my spirit home, but they had only come to encourage me in my perilous position. We lay there in the wet and shivered all night and it looks unreasonable to say, when it was daylight that we could stand on our feet. Tremblingly I could say, "Oh Lord, thou hast brought up my soul from the grave. Thou hast kept me alive, that I should not go down into the pit." Psalms xxx, 3rd verse. As soon as it was light we started again on our march, though we were faint, weak and sore. We soon heard a negro calling hogs. We pressed our weary steps toward him as rapidly as possible, but lo, we soon saw when we went near, that we could get no corn there without being seen. Therefore we were compelled to travel on about four miles, around a large farm and across another dense swamp and crossing it we immediately came to a corn field and negro peas. We grabed peas and filled our mouths until we got some corn husked, and then sat down and ate three ears apiece in less than twenty minutes. This was about the first time we had sat down to eat. While here we soon heard the hounds coming up the swamp. We resolved if they pursued us we would slay them with clubs.

When we found that they had passed our tracks, we felt as though we were safe, at least, for a while, we supposed they were after a fox; we soon resumed our march. The corn we had been eating was dry and hard; we traveled on around the plantation and presently came to a house, the yard was full of little rebs playing, and between the fence and the house there was a late roasting-ear patch; the corn was in good roasting-ear, C. E. Tibbles and I said we would have some of that soft corn, and over the fence we went, our haversacks were soon filled, which was indeed a treat to us—we passed on and soon were in a dense forest and wilderness of brush and green briers, a feasting on our raw corn. It was a feast indeed. No picnic dinner ever tasted so good to me. God blessed it and kept us by his power.

One evening about dusk we felt as though we were in a critical place, we soon found a negro that informed us that rebs were thick going through the country and we concluded to seek a place to hide until a late hour, so we slipped up to an old fodder-house and went in. It was about one hundred yards from the house; and in a short time a great racket commenced at the house and we could discover men maneuvering around the house; we did not shut our eyes, for we were taught to watch as well as pray. We supposed they were having a rebel hoedown, but we had no idea of taking part with them. However we discovered a squad approaching us, we supposed they intended to press us into the service; but as they neared the fodder-house door we leaped out of the window, which was in the back part of the fodder-house. We were soon out in the swamps. It was Egyptian darkness. In a short time after we struck the road and was going along we heard the clatter of sabres and horses feet. It was the rebel cavalry; they came in hearing so suddenly that we leaped about fifteen feet and lay down in the brush until they passed and got up and again resumed our journey.

It soon began to rain and continued on until the next evening, and as it was still raining, we had had no chance to get any corn to eat. We were drenched with the rain, and were starving and dying by inches. We now happened to hear a negro coming through the woods singing. George Tibbles said if we would stop and remain where we were, he would go and see if that negro could give us aid, by helping or giving us something to eat, and by telling us how to cross the large river that we were now approaching. But the negro told him that they could not get enough to eat themselves; and he would be glad to help us if he could. But he informed us how to cross the river; so we went down an old by-road, the rain falling in torrents, and we were staggering with weakness and were nearly exhausted, and would have given up and died, but life seemed dear to us for we wanted to see our friends, and be buried with God's people. The sufferings of this night will never be erased from my memory. We toiled on through the Egyptian darkness, water, mud and rain, until we came to the river, and was there piloted across by a negro; as soon as we were on the other side we found a patch of corn, and were soon feasting upon it. Shortly afterward we found another negro, and he said they had killed a hog a few days ago and had not eaten it because it was somewhat spoiled, and he would sell us a piece. So we bought about one pound and it was green and slick. But we gave him a five dollar bill for it, and ate it with our corn.

One day we were traveling through the swamps, and we saw two other men that had made their escape from prison, and as we approached another river, these two men said they intended to go to the bridge to cross. We crossed the rivers generally wherever we came to them, for we shunned the bridges for fear of the rebels. We told them we wouldn't go, but they went, and in a few minutes after they left us we heard a volley of musketry in the direction of the bridge, and as we never saw or heard of them again, we supposed they were shot by rebel guards.

CHAPTER XIV.

G. N. Tibbles Finds One Large Sweet Potato—Still on the Tramp and Meet a Rebel Negro—Home at Last—The Prisoner's Lament.

WE came to a river one day that we were afraid to cross. We wandered along the bank dreading it, for we were so weak, and the river so wide and swift, and seemed to be full of whirlpools that would take a man under. Finally we concluded that we *must* cross, so we stripped off all our clothes, and done them up in as small a bundle as we could, then C. E. Tibbles, being an expert swimmer, leaped into the foaming waters, swam to the middle of the river and dropped down, but could not touch bottom there, but hunted around and finally found a place where the two of us that could not swim could cross by leaping up and jumping and so we crossed with great difficulty. When Davis, from New York was nearly across he began to sink, but George Tibbles caught him and helped him out and thereby saved his life.

We toiled on through the swamps until we were exhausted, weary and nearly fainting, fell in despair. It seemed as though we could find no cornfield, and G. N. Tibbles said in a whisper to us to stay there, and he would go and see if *he* could not find something for us to eat, and he went and returned with *one large sweet potato*. We ate part of it, and saved the rest to eat with raw corn. We ran across a negro that day and asked him for information, and he said he was a rebel. We urged him not to say anything about seeing us, he said he would not if we didn't want him to; we assured

6

him we were his friends. As soon as he was out of sight we
raised the double-quick, and went for miles into the dismal
swamps, for we felt more safe when we were away down in
the dense wilderness of swamp brush and greenbriers, for we
had hid in them so long. Every fright we would get, we
would run for miles so we could get into these low down
swamps, though when there we would famish and faint for
food and water before we could get out. However, we aimed
to travel in the swamps altogether in the day time, but sometimes we would pass over some dry land. We got one mess
of little hard apples on the entire trip, and I often wondered
that they did not kill us, for they were so poor and hard and
we ate so greedily of them; and we had one mess of water-
melons, and one mess of tame grapes, which we picked off a
man's porch. We were so near starved to death we ran
right through the yard and soon filled ourselves with the
grapes. O, how delicious they were, and how we feasted upon
them, and then filled our haversacks with the grapes, and
feeling refreshed we again resumed our weary march onward.
Now in the lone swamps there were no wild grapes, and when
on the dry land, we could get corn and would not take the
time to bother with them.

The rebels did not have any pickets on the south side of
their camps, they just had scouts. One night we were traveling with all the speed that we possibly could and about three
o'clock in the morning we found ourselves in the rebel camp;
we went up to their artillery and then turned and intended to
go around the infantry, when lo, we found ourselves in the
midst of the rebel infantry camp. Now we were somewhat
confused, but we hurried right on through their camp, and if
they saw us they took us for their own men, (but they were

greatly fooled if they did.) We went on safe through and
coming out in the main road a ways, we soon discovered a
picket fire and slipped up until we were within ten steps of
the picket; we could see every man, just how they were situated; we soon fell back a proper distance, and concluded if
they would let us alone that we would serve them the same
way, and so started double-quick through the brush, and
we traveled for about four miles down the Flint river bottom.
What a terrible dangerous place this river was, but we did not
hesitate long, but went in and soon crossed over the waving,
dangerous water. It was now about sun-rise and when
we landed our hearts sank within us at the terrible swamp
that lay before us; despair, starvation and death was pictured
in every countenance, but we, weak and trembling, entered
the swamp. It was rather dry at this time, there were tall
green briers with both ends in the ground, swamp brush, and
the vines were so dense that it was next to impossible to pen-
etrate it. Our limbs were all cut, and bleeding, and swollen;
and our clothing was torn to ribbons and strings. As sore
as we were, we were compelled to get down on all fours and
crawl for almost half a day, and then we could see no light;
we finally came to a bush about forty feet in height and I
climbed up it to see if I could see any light or open space in
the swamp.

But I could not discover any. There seemed to be paths
all through this swamp made by wild vermin and beasts.
Though it seemed impossible for a very large beast to get
through without getting their nose right on the ground and
creeping along the same as we did. Our knees and hands
were all cut and bleeding with briers and thorns until it was
next to impossible for us to walk at all, in fact it was suffer-

ing beyond reason for us. But it was life or death with us. To stop was death, to be recaptured was death, and to be discovered by a citizen was the same, while perseverance was life. After I came down from the tree we again resumed our march on all fours, but were surprised when we soon came to a steep bluff. Now I will describe those green briers of which I have spoken, for we had to travel through them so much. Well they were about the size of a man's finger. They grow in low swampy ground and are always green; they grow from ten to thirty feet long, and run like vines over the swamp bushes and frequently both ends fasten in the ground. It was they that tore our cloths and flesh so while running from the hounds. We now ascended the hill weary and faint for we had been in this dry hot swamp so long without water or food. We now started out on a trot through a dense forest, like wild beasts and traveled nearly all day before coming to any corn field, where we could get some to eat. The country now became more rough and hilly, sometimes a dense swamp and sometimes hills. About dusk one evening we were in a perfect wilderness, we ran under a dense cluster of vines that hung about four feet above the ground and formed a good house under there, so thick when once in we could not see out. We darted under there, when lo, there was a prisoner who had come from Florence prison all alone. He soon left us and the next morning we heard a volley of musketry. We thought he had ran into a rebel picket and was shot for we never heard of him getting through and he was aiming for the same point that we were.

The poor fellow struggled, toiled and suffered to save his life, then was compelled to lose it without seeing his friends. We now discovered a negro, and being desirous of learning the distance to the Neuse river, sought an opportunity to talk with him which we did, and he informed us that as soon as we got to the Stone river we would be safe, for he said the Yanks were guarding the bridge. We now felt somewhat encouraged, as the river was only some thirty miles distant. We were soon there, but would not venture to go on the bridge, and aimed some three miles below it, for we were afraid to trust the darkey too far; I don't think he meant to mislead us, but when we got to the river, we could look up it and see the rebs walking on the bridge. We were now so near the Union lines, that without a doubt had we gone there we would have been shot; and the country was full of bushwhackers. When we started across the river we got nearly across when we sunk in the quick sand and nearly perished, but finally worked our way out. We found that our troops had fallen back across the Neuse river, which left us in the midst of the bushwhackers. We finally decided to go to the road, thinking we might come to the Union pickets. Once into the road we could see northern papers, oyster and sardine cans that had come from the north. O, what joy even those emblems gave us. Hope now sprang up within us and we exclaimed within our hearts: "Why art thou cast down, O, my soul, and why art thou disquieted within me? Hope in God; for I shall yet praise Him who is the health of my countenance, and my God."

With light hearts we now traveled on with all the speed we possibly could the remainder of that day, the night following and also the next day until about noon. We were expecting to come to our picket guards every minute; and were now so excited with the hope of seeing our pickets, that we did not take time to hunt any corn to eat, so we traveled twenty-four hours without anything to eat. It seemed like we were so close to the Union lines and to liberty, that the very air seemed changed, but it was a perilous place for us in the midst of rebel scouts and bushwhackers, but we felt that we were under God's protecting care. Not even a bird could flit by unnoticed by us, or a man come near without our notice in sufficient time to escape from danger or death. I now ventured up to the gate of a large farm house where I saw an aged couple sitting on a porch, and I asked the old gentleman how far it was to the Neuse river. He replied it was about two miles; but he took us for rebs, and said: Don't go there, for the Yankees are thick along the river." I then asked if that was the nearest point to the river, and he replied, " No; it was only about one mile across the fields, but we had better keep away from the river, for the Yanks were so thick scouting up and down the river on the other side, that it was very dangerous to go near the river. Dear reader, you cannot imagine how our poor hearts were delighted to think we were so close to friends and food.

We took across the plantation with all the energy we could command until we came to the long looked for river, with eager eyes we penetrated the forest on the other side, but could see no blue coats or Union men; but there lies before us a great deep river, a mile wide. We wandered up and down looking in vain, with eager eyes, trying to catch a glimpse of a blue coat on the other shore; we were so anxious to get transport over the river. The evening's shade was now drawing its curtains around us, and we feared every moment that we would be shot by bushwackers. C. E. Tibbles and G. N. Tibbles, being expert swimmers, got a flat rail and got on it and launched out in the deep and landed safe on the other shore where friends and kindred dwell, where the land flows with good provisions. Davis now thought he would cross on a rail, but just as he started out the rail turned and he would have perished in the deep water had I not assisted him in getting back to the shore. We were now hungry, weak and faint and almost ready to despair. Just at dusk we saw a darky and he told us to go four miles down the river to a mill, and we would find a Union man, but he said in all probability we would get shot before we got there, however he gave us as safe a route to go as he could. So weary and faint and weak as we were we toiled on until nine o'clock when we reached a large mill, but no dwelling house and no light was visible, but we rapped on the mill door; no sound was heard within, we listened in vain for a footfall until our hearts almost ceased to beat; we arose and attempted to go a little further although it was in a staggering manner with starvation and weakness; when we went a little distance we looked across the river, when lo! we discovered a bright picket fire, with blue coats standing around it. That sight was like the morning star of hope to us. So we again made way to the mill door and pounded upon it with all the power we had; shortly a foot step was heard within and a voice said "Who is there?" I replied "a friend I guess." So in a short time the door was opened by a large old negro. We soon told him a brief history of ourselves and the old darkey shouted and praised God for our deliverance. We were soon taken through the mill back into a little old hut and was given coffee, cold potatoes and meat to eat—but very little done us. He spread down some quilts in the mill for us to lie down upon—how thankful we felt for even these. As soon as the break of day the old darkey came to us.

Although I had not slept any during the night, for that Union picket fire and the blue coats was before my eyes all night long; for that fire was the Star of Hope, life and liberty to me. The old darkey told us to come now before it was clear light, for if the rebs should see us there it would be death to us and himself also; so we were soon rowed across the river by a *stout* young negro—and as soon as we could we made our way to Uncle Sam's boys' camp. There was a New York regiment on the outer guard, and as we went into camp they fell into line and gave three cheers for the Fourth Iowa.

There is no pen nor even tongue that could describe my feelings, to realize that I was free and among friends. The colonel gave us a glass of brandy; the chaplain pinned our rags up as best he could to hide our nakedness until we could get some clothing. Breakfast was soon prepared for us but we could eat but a few bits, we were so near starved to death, that it seemed we could not eat. Now this was all done for us by a New York regiment, whom we never had seen before. But they felt as near and dear to us as any brother could feel toward another. It was now the first day of October, 1864, and we were six miles from Newbern, N. C. The Colonel soon ordered a team to take us to Newbern and as we four prisoners rode along my heart was filled with praise to God who had so miraculously delivered us from death by the hand of our enemies. Surely I could say in the language of the Psalmist, 20th chapter, 6th verse, " Now know I that the Lord saveth his annointed; He will hear from his holy heaven, with the saving strength of his right hand. I will bless the Lord who has given me council. Psalm 16 chap., 10th verse. We were soon in Newbern, furnished with good quarters, clothing and good food. But as soon as we were quiet and our excitement over we were helpless. Our feet and legs swollen and we were weak we could scarcely walk across the room. The yellow fever was now raging in Newbern; the people were dying at the rate of sixty per day. We remained four days until we were able to walk around some and then were sent by rail to Morehead City, N. C., on coast. Here we stayed one day and gathered oysters in the shell on the coast. We then got aboard of a ship and sailed for Fortress Monroe, Va., and when within five miles of that city, a tug boat met us with a physician on board; they would not let us land for sixteen days on account of yellow fever being on the ship. The doctor brought us five days' rations and another suit of clothing and the ship sailed on for New York City were we met the same resistance as before. During our voyage there we were in great peril by a heavy storm and thought we would all be drowned. Oh, the raging fury; how it tossed our ship around and how sickening the thought, that after having undergone so much suffering, privations, and to be spared to get so near home and yet never reach there, but the same hand that had preserved us in the past troubles, calmed the roaring sea and we were enabled to stem the storm and again cast anchor at New York City, and by a little intrigue, we prisoners got on board of a tug boat and sailed to shore. We had now been sailing six days and nights without seeing land. I got very sick at first but finally got better. We landed in New York City, October 12, 1864. We were directed to a soldiers' home, the first I had ever seen and I had soldiered three years. The home was but a short distance from the boat landing, but we were so weak and trembling that it was with great difficulty that we reached there. But here we received good attention and care for two days and then took rail for Buffalo, New York.

Here we were nursed with great care for two days, and thence we were sent to Cincinnati, Ohio; here we were stopped for two days more, and then sent on to Cleveland, Ohio, and remained a few days. We now began to realize that we were gaining some strength. We were shown the greatest kindness, and everything was furnished us that was calculated to give us strength and build us up, wherever we were sent. We stopped at all the main cities along the road home, and recruited our health and strength. We boys then separated, each to return to his respective home. The Tibbles boys and I had been together so long that it was with feelings of sadness that we separated. I then went to Keokuk, Iowa, and stopped; the people gathered around me as they would around Gen. Grant, and gave me good and kind attention, and even money was presented me. I then left for Winterset, Iowa, arriving there, at "my old home," November 1, 1864. My friends had all given me up for *dead*. The Tibbles boys' widowed mother had even had their funerals preached, and some of my friends were contemplating the same ; and O! the joy and sweet pleasure in our again being permitted to meet in this world was better felt than described. I now reported myself to Des Moines, and the Provost Marshal ordered me to return home until my health got better, and when I got able to travel, to report to Davenport, Iowa, and get my discharge. I was now able to go to church, and enjoy the society of young folks; and, on the 25th day of December, 1864, I was united in marriage to Miss E. J. Bowlsby, of Winterset, Madison County, Iowa, in Osceola, Iowa, by Rev. A. S. Elliott; and on January 3, 1865, I was honorably discharged from the United States service at Davenport, Iowa. I quit chewing tobacco, and have never again resumed the filthy practice. I now settle down in life with weak lungs and a broken constitution, and when the war broke out I was counted one among the stoutest men in the county; but the sufferings, hardships and exposures to which I was subjected while in the employ of Uncle Sam, has left me but a wreck of my former self. But, nevertheless, it is a miracle wrought by the Divine hand on me that I am alive, and it is through His mercy alone that I live to-day. God is just.

THE PRISONER'S LAMENT.

When our country called for men,
We came from forge and store and mill—
From workshop, farm and factory,
The broken ranks to fill.
We left our quiet, happy homes,
And others we loved so well,
To vanquish all the Union foes,
Or fall where others fell.
Now in prisons drear we languish,
And it is our constant cry —
Oh, ye! who yet can save us,
Why leave us here to die?

The tongue of slander tells you
That our hearts were filled with fear —
That all or nearly all of us
Were captured in the rear;
But the scars upon our bodies
Of musket ball and shell,
The missing legs and shattered arms,
A truer tale will tell.

We have tried to do our duty
In the sight of *God* on high —
Oh, ye ! who yet can save us,
Why leave us here to die ?

There are hearts with hope still beating,
In each pleasant Northern home —
Watching, waiting for the loved ones
 Who may *never, never* come.
 Meager, tattered, pale and gaunt;
Growing weaker every day
With pinching cold and want,
Brothers, sons and husbands lay —
Poor and helpless and captured they lie —
Oh, ye! who yet can save us,
Why will you leave us here to die?

Outside, yet near Andersonville prison gates,
There is a graveyard close at hand,
Where lie thirteen thousand Union men
Beneath the Georgia sand.
Scores are added daily,
As day succeeds each day ;
And thus it will be ever
Until all have passed away.
The last can say, when dying,
With upturned and glazing eye,
Both Love and Faith are dead at home,
Else why leave us here to die?

This was the lamentation of hundreds as they passed from
Andersonville to that bourne from which no traveler returns.

But before bringing my history to a final close, I wish to
say that in the spring of 1861 there were in the loyal states
4,000,000 men fit for military duty or service, and over 2,000,-
000 volunteered for service against the rebellion; and there

were of this number 96,000 killed in action, 5,000 of which were commissioned officers, and there were 183,000 died of disease. Total, 279,000, and there were 1,300 died in Andersonville prison, the total number of prisoners who died during the war of the rebellion is 36,401. Comrades, this calls our attention to the thousands of our brave comrades that were slaughtered by our sides, and of the sufferings and privations through which we passed during the rebellion. It was our nation's best men that crowded the ranks of the Union army, and we can but pay our tribute to those who fell in the defense of liberty, and to whose sacrifice we owe all the blessings which we now enjoy. The scenes of those years of war and carnage are engraved on memory's page as with a pen of iron. They stand out like the lightning track on the dark back ground of night. We could not forget them if we would. Nor should they be forgotten. They are gone. Is this all? Is the end in material things? Shall we never see our soldiers again? Shall we never walk with them on the shores beyond the river? Is there no hope beyond the grave? In a few days we too, will be called. Already our locks are whitening. If this be all of it; if the grave is the end, then it is questionable whether they have not paid too dearly for these blessings we enjoy. But it is not the end. Things present are typical of things to come. Analogies reign, and things seen aid in the interpretation of things unseen. Is there no hope that we shall bloom out into brighter and more glorious beings. Comrades, the long roll will soon be sounded for another muster. Are you ready to fall in? Can we expect to spend a life in selfishness and sin, and then give to heaven the drugs and dross of it. Can we expect to muster unless we make preparations for it? Comrades, if we will fall in line and obey our Commander, we will come off conqueror through Him that loved us to the enjoyment of a happy and brighter resting place beyond the grave with all the pure and good. "God is love."   Yours truly,

J. R. COMPTON,
Company F, Fourth Iowa Volunteer Infantry.

CHAPTER XV.

Capture of Jeff Davis—"My Old Mother."

"Strike! till the last armed foe expires;
Strike! for your altars and your fires;
Strike! for the green graves of your sires,
God and your native land.

I WILL now give you a minute history of the capture of Jeff Davis, in addition to my experience. Davis at the approach of danger hurried southward, leaving to Lee and the remnant of his army the task of defending the State of Virginia. On the third of April he arrived in Danville and assumed, with such of his cabinet and officials as he could gather around him, to establish the fiction of a government; he also issued a proclamation announcing his intention to hold on to Virginia, but the capitulation of Lee and the threatening aspect of Sherman and Stoneman, counseled him to move further southward, while his escape was possible, with his fugitive government fast crumbling to pieces around him; he still maintained an appearance of confidence, and a degree of assurance which deceived no one; and at Charlotta, North Carolina, where he remained several days, he made a public speech, promising soon to have a larger army than ever before in the field. About April 25th, he left Charlotta, alarmed by the approach of Stoneman's cavalry, who now became aware that the great head of the rebellion was in their neighborhood. Passing through Yorkville, South Carolina, with a train of several ambulances and a small mounted escort he entered Georgia in the beginning of May, and on the 31st reached Washington, a small town northwest of Augusta, thence he moved rapidly southward, hoping, possibly, to reach the Gulf and there find a vessel to convey him to Cuba. Meanwhile rumors of the flight of Davis through Georgia, reached General Wilson at Macon, who sent out parties of cavalry to scour the neighboring country; at Irvingsville, about seventy miles south of Macon, the Fourth Michigan Cavalry, Colonel Pritchard, came upon traces of the Rebel Ex-President, two miles outside the town; they were completely surprised and the whole party of fugitives captured, including Mrs. Davis and her sister, the Rebel Postmaster-General Reagan and others.

The following description of the manner in which Davis was captured is vouched for as true to the minutest detail, by an eye witness : Andrew Bee, a private of Company L, went to the entrance of Davis's tent and was met by Mrs. Davis, bareheaded and barefoot, who, putting her hand on his arm, said : "Please do not go in there till my daughter gets herself dressed." Andrew thereupon drew back, and in a few minutes a young lady (Miss Howell) and another person, bent over as with age, wearing a lady's water-proof gathered at the waist, with a shawl drawn over the head, and carrying a tin pail, appeared and asked to go to the run for water. Mrs. Davis also appears and says: "For God's sake, let my old mother go to get some water." No objections being made, they passed out, but sharp eyes were upon the singular old mother. Suddenly, Corporal Munger, of Company C, and others at the same instant, noticed that the old mother was wearing very heavy boots for an aged female, and the corporal exclaimed, "That is not a woman ! Don't you see the boots?" and spurring his horse forward and cocking his carbine, compelled the withdrawal of the shawl, and disclosed Jeff. Davis. As if stung by this discovery of his unmanliness, Jeff. struck an attitude and cried out: "*Is there a man among you? If there is, let me see him.*" "*Yes,*" said the corporal, "*I am one, and if you stir, I will blow your brains out.*" "I know my fate, and might as well die here." But his wife threw her arms around his neck and kept herself between him and the threatening corporal. No harm was done him, and he was generally kindly spoken to ; he was only stripped of his female attire. As a man, he was dressed in a complete suit of grey, a light felt hat and high cavalry boots, with a grey beard of about six weeks' growth covering his face. He said he thought our government was too magnanimous to hunt women and children in that way.. When Col. Pritchard told him he would do the best he could for his comfort. he answered, "I ask no favors of you." To which surly reply the colonel courteously responded by assuring him of kind treatment. "He ought to have fallen in the hands of some man that had suffered in Andersonville prison about six months. I don't think Jeff would have been quite so saucy, or he soon would have wilted."

Davis was conveyed to Macon and thence to Fortress Monroe, where he arrived in the latter part of May, and where he was incarcerated, awaiting his trial for high treason. Stevens, the rebel Vice-President, was captured about the same time, together with others who had held high civil and military positions in the rebel government. On June, 1865, there was not an organized body of men east of the Rio Grande who defied the authority of the national government. On May

7

23d and 24th, the armies of Grant and Sherman were re-
viewed in Washington, in the presence of President Johnson
and a vast concourse of people. The United States at once
took its place among the great powers of the world more
than ever before.

INDEX.

CHAPTER I.

CHAPTER II.

CHAPTER III.

CHAPTER IV.

CHAPTER V.

CHAPTER VI.

CHAPTER VII.